DRINKE

— AT THE —

SPRING

— OF —

KARDAKI

For Gerry, Mark and Finny, with love,
and
in memoriam, Louis

DRINKER
AT THE
SPRING
OF
KARDAKI

LINDA
MᶜNAMARA

WOLFHOUND PRESS

First published 1992 by
Wolfhound Press
68 Mountjoy Square,
Dublin 1

Wolfhound Press receives financial assistance from The Arts Council / An
Chomhairle Ealaíon, Dublin, Ireland.

This book is fiction. All characters, incidents and names have no connection with
any persons, living or dead. Any apparent resemblance is purely coincidental.

British Library Cataloguing in Publication Data
McNamara, Linda
    Drinker at the Spring of Kardaki
    I. Title
    823.914 [FS]

    ISBN 0-86327-333-5

With acknowledgements to *The Irish Press* 'New Irish Writing', *KRINO*, *Passages*,
The Salmon, RTE Radio and BBC Radio, where some of these stories first appeared.

Cover design and illustration: Peter Haigh
Typesetting: Wolfhound Press
Printed in Great Britain by Cox & Wyman Ltd, Reading, Berkshire

CONTENTS

DRINKER AT
THE SPRING OF KARDAKI

I

It began one Friday afternoon in February. At four-thirty I swept together the loose papers on my desk and leaned into the curved comfort of my chair, staring through the smeared window panes. Outside, the light was almost gone and the haggard faces of warehouses and lofts across the road were already filled with shadows. It had been a cold and clear day: above the roofs, night unrolled the first sprinkling of pale stars.

'Tom, is that report cleared yet?'

My section head glanced up from her desk beneath the window and studied my attitude of repose.

'Yes,' I said, 'it's all ready. In fact, Sheila's down at the photocopier now.'

'Good. Just make sure there are plenty of spare copies.'

There was a slight pause and I sat forward a little, until she nodded in acknowledgement and turned back to her own tasks. I relaxed again and sank into the padded plastic, stretching my legs beneath the desk. There was no real danger that I would be allocated a new job this late in the day, so far down the span of the week: she was a fair supervisor, realising that the effort I had made to reach the deadline merited an hour of relaxation. Most of us in the room had worked hard on the report over the past four days, skipping tea-breaks and cutting short lunch hours, earning an end of week hiatus. It was a hardworking section, anxious to achieve targets whenever they were realistic, and she recognised that effort.

So, as Sheila returned, unfolding her armful of spare photocopies onto my desk and gazing at me anxiously, I cleared my throat.

'Anna?'

'Um?'

'Sheila's off home this weekend — she'll need to head for the train ....'

'What? Oh — of course. Off you go now, Sheila, there's a good girl, or you'll be late. And — thanks.'

Sheila smiled gratefully at us both as she pushed her chair tidily against her small desk and rushed out with coat and case.

When the door had shut on the frantic rustles of the corridor, silence swelled to fill the office. Padraic, the final member of the section, had been gone since lunchtime, sacrificing half a day's leave to beat the country-bound traffic. His desk was bare except for a pen and a ruler; it faced blankly the more cluttered neatness of Sheila's corner. Anna was reading, but the turning of the pages made no sound.

It was only four minutes to five, according to my watch: I had over half-an-hour before the day was finished. I could, of course, leave early. Unlike Sheila, I was senior enough not to have to ask permission: it had already been acknowledged that my work for the week was done. But if I stayed sitting at my desk until the precise time for finishing up, I could catch the usual bus, see exactly the same fellow passengers as on every other day; above all, in the free space of the next half-hour, I could carry out my periodic review of my working environment, the items dotted around the surface of my desk, the riot of staples and rubber bands in the top left-hand drawer.

I am an organised person, almost obsessively so, at work and at home (in this I am different from Maeve — it is among the chief of our complementary divergences). My office is exemplary. The pot plants which I have purchased from time to time over the past few years are situated on top of the filing cabinet beside Anna to catch optimal amounts of light and heat — in summer, from the old casement window and, in winter, from the fluorescent lights and the gurgling radiator.

My desk itself, tucked into a corner of the rectangular room beside the door, holds two ordered trays: that labelled 'IN', from which I select each morning my day's tasks, and that labelled 'OUT', into which I place a succession of completed items, until the last flops into place at about five twenty-five each evening.

The order of all this is not only pleasing to me: I consider it essential if the tasks of the office are to be completed in a satisfactory manner. In an organisation overwhelmed by paper, my section is remarkable for the speed with which papers are filed and the ease with which they can be retrieved again if called for.

As their supervisor, I see it as my responsibility to instil proper management habits into Sheila and Padraic: the gap in our ages and the fact that they are both new to the organisation make this a relatively easy task. Anna's corner is a sad example, but then she is the boss and she can, in a matter of moments, disembarrass herself of the chaos by passing an armful of paper in my direction. Anna's untidiness does not annoy me: in her complete inability to cope she reminds me of Maeve, and I have long ago come to terms with the disorder Maeve leaves in her wake.

I am, if I say so myself, a model supervisor and quite a tractable member of my section. Any aggression I may feel or have felt from time to time towards my superiors in this office has never been occasioned by their personalities — I have been very lucky in the succession of people who have inhabited the bright corner by the window — but rather by their organisational rank. The denizens of the highest rooms in our office block have, you understand, in their elite wisdom decided to slide their fingertips down past my name on the various occasions when promotional opportunities opened up. As a result, it has taken me an unconscionably long time to move up from the small table and straight chair, which are all that a Sheila or a Padraic merit, to my present position. But still my wooden desk and soft seat, however polished and curved, are somewhat less imposing and inhabit a bleaker corner of the room than those possessed by Anna — a woman of good looks and some intelligence, no doubt, but one who is ten years my junior in the service of the organisation.

I am not alone, you must understand: there are the high flyers and the low flyers, and there are almost as many of us as of them. But we do not experience solidarity, we the low flyers: instead we avoid each other's eye in the corridors and castigate each other's rumoured failings at tea-breaks. We are all anxious for dissociation, terrified that contact with the others, the true downtrodden, will hinder rectification of the understandable mistake which has resulted in our own temporary miscasting.

That Friday afternoon, telepathy must have been at work. As I shuffled and aligned the edges of the spare reports, I was thinking of my last interview with one of the dwellers on the pyramid's apex. Although occurring two years previously, it still returned to me as crisp as actuality, whenever I wished to recall it.

I had not been nervous while the lift carried me upwards or as I then waited in the ante-room. I was too absorbed in the rituals of the upper floors, in observing the young secretary guard the flickering console on her desk and in committing to memory the other trappings of power, the pale-green walls, the white mock-Georgian mouldings.

A red light blazed and died on the console and the girl immediately said, 'He'll see you now — just go straight in.'

In my mind, I again advanced to the heavy polished door, but this time I stopped to make a jocular remark which would cause the secretary to blush the colour of her nail polish; I tried now to think of suitable words, but failed and left it for a future session of reflection, impatient to reach the crucial stages of the drama.

While I bent to store the bundle of photocopies in the lower drawer of my desk and snapped it shut, I was hearing in my memory the softer click of my entrance to the sanctum. At that precise instant — and this is what I mean by telepathy — the office door behind me burst open, startling both Anna and myself into upright positions.

Anna had the advantage of facing the door, so it was not until I saw the smile of obeisance latch itself to her face and he was halfway across the room that I recognised my old interviewer, making a rare descent from the top of the building. As he bent and showed Anna a thick document, and a yellow memo slip, murmuring instructions, I felt disquieted at the urgency of his gestures. When he left, he passed my desk with a moue of almost-greeting, perfected over the years of ascent through the slippery passages of this and other organisations.

As the door shut behind him, Anna was looking at her watch, then at me.

'Tom, I know it's late — but they have to have another three copies of the survey this evening.'

As she returned to her seat, she was impassive, but the memo slip had suddenly displaced her desultory reading and her face blanched under the neon lighting. I guessed that she had received an equally urgent but more complex set of instructions on her own behalf. For her sake, I swallowed my annoyance at the lateness and the indignity of the task as I flicked through the document on my way to the door: there were almost thirty pages to be done.

'Shall I bring them upstairs?'

'No, you can leave them back with me. I'll be going up there later on.'

It was exactly five fifteen by the clock over the lift as I hurried past to the photocopier. I briefly regretted having let Sheila slip off early; if we had been able to divide the document, the job would have taken only a few minutes. But, in any case, she and Padraic would already have left by five fifteen for their rural weekends, in the vanguard of the crowd jostling past me and down the stairs in preference to enduring the slowness of the lift's passage.

I resolutely turned my back on them and watched the machine hiccup and grind into life. It seemed as unhappy as I was to be pressed into service at such a late hour. As I automatically switched the pages, lifting and shutting the cover, then watching the flash, flash, flash through the gap at the hinges, I seethed at the disruption to my evening. Now I would miss my bus, and probably the one after that as well; for the sake of ten minutes' delay in arriving at the stop, I could be as much as an hour late getting home through the peak traffic.

The copier seemed to pause now and again, as if more worn out than ever at the end of a week's service, and I felt it might at any moment break down. Once, the machinery did falter and stop, with a fearful rending, but it was only a sheet of paper that had paid for being a millimetre out of line and was immediately consumed by the rollers; I knew, from thirty years of similar incidents, how to extract the shredded inky pages and begin again.

Someone had taped a travel poster onto the wall behind the machine, whether in a spirit of benevolence or from an urge to torment by way of contrast with the viewer's situation, I could not decide. It was a large picture of a Greek church, luminous under a sky of a colour I had never seen elsewhere, unless it was in photographs of the same place. On this particular evening in February, it seemed to mock my immediate preoccupations, serenely desolate under cloudless blue, and I shivered as the draught up the stairwell caught me at the back of the ankles.

I don't know if it was then that I decided, or after the stapler slipped and tore my hand, and I saw the stragglers on their way down smile at my words. Perhaps it was later, after I had handed Anna the papers and left her hemmed in by them, scribbling to her reflection in the now black window-pane, her abstracted shuffling the only sound in the building as I slipped my coat on.

'Thanks a million, Tom. Have a good weekend, now.'

'Same to you. Bye ....'

Although it was only seven minutes past the half-hour, the corridors were dim on emergency lighting and rows of doors hung half-open, revealing the grey, pathetic shapes of abandoned office furniture. It was almost as if I had slipped into a time warp as I trod carefully along the edge of the carpeting, touching the walls now and again with my fingertips to orient myself. The lower orders, those who normally filled the corridors with noise and colour, might have left years rather than minutes previously. No echo, no odour of their passing lingered in the thickly insulated stairways, and the cleaning staff had not yet arrived to shatter the illusion with their booming machines and the sharp tang of freshly splashed disinfectant.

Outside, gazing upward from the opposite side of the street, I could make out Anna's lonely light and, above that, the shining windows of my one time interviewer's office. The next casement along, that of his antechamber, was blank, and for a moment I entertained a fantasy in which I prowled through the darkness between the furniture towards the inner sanctum, there to enact an alternative, more favourable, outcome to my real interview. But such thoughts soon passed from me: I do not let myself indulge in them too long or too often. I could not maintain my equanimity, my tidiness, if I did not censor my emotions. As I lowered my eyes to street level, I saw my bus pulling irretrievably away from the stop; it was a punishment of sorts, you might say.

The travel agent's window that I leaned into, out of the bitter wind, had always been there. What made me look into it that night is, in retrospect, quite difficult to determine: a combination of factors, none of which seems to stand out. At the time, however, I imagine that I thought only of the poster behind the photocopier. After all, the plastic banner suctioned onto the glass from the inside proclaimed *Greek Holidays our Speciality*, and I had never been to Greece.

The inside of the shop was chillier than I expected, the temperature lowered by the constantly clanging door, and the staff behind the brochure-spattered counter wore thick jumpers and scarves wrapped around their necks, perhaps to counterpoint the bright sunshine depicted around them. I waited among the other customers, turning up my coat collar and looking at the posters on the wall. Yugoslavia, Spain and Morocco blended into an indistinguishable swathe of sea and sand. My eyes, familiar with this pattern from previous years, unfocused.

'Yes, sir?'

I had become the next in line too quickly; I had to make an effort to recall and give voice to my request.

'I'm interested in something, umm, Greek. Do you have any spare brochures?'

'Well ... there are several available, actually. What sort of thing had you in mind — classical, island-hopping? Perhaps a combination holiday?'

The man facing me was numbed by all the possibilities. A glazed look came into his eyes as he realised I was at the indecisive stage. To avoid his disdain, I stared at the rack behind him.

'Um ... could I take that one there, at the top on the right?'

On the cover of the brochure I had chosen there was a near replica of the poster: a white bulbous church from a different angle, another section of empty indigo stratosphere.

'Of course,' he said, relieved, leaning back to snatch my choice from its brethern before I could change my mind. 'You might like to look at this one as well — it's slightly less expensive, but it still has the day flights.'

'Thanks. You seem to be very busy tonight.'

I offered the remark to delay my exit from the tepid atmosphere of the shop into the chiller night air. Then I saw through the window that the queue at my stop was gathering stragglers and beginning to shuffle — an indication that a bus was rounding the corner.

When I had reached the top of the long queue, there were seats left only on the top deck, but tonight I did not notice the acrid pall of cigarette smoke which draped itself under the curved ceiling, conscious only of a more incense-like intoxication from the burgeoning illustrations of the brochures as I turned over the pages, making my choice.

Things would be different this year, I decided after I had closed the brochures, no more vacillation or nights poring over our collection of photo albums. I knew that Maeve would be relieved, since she could never make out which captions went with which pictures, despite my patient explanations. This time, perhaps because it would be the first without our newly independent son, she had not even mentioned the subject of holidays. No, the planning of the summer fortnight was really my responsibility, just as the arrangement of the post-holiday prints had always been my particular ritual.

Each year in January, when the sun had not been seen for long weeks, the albums would be pulled from their box in the bottom half of the bookcase and slid around on the sittingroom floor until Danny pounced on one at random and began to ask questions. In the lull between the early news and the evening film, after the tea things had been cleared away into the dishwasher, we would sit around the fire and turn the stiff pages. Maeve would crouch on a stool, ignoring the labels I had typed and stuck beneath each photo, and struggle aloud to identify elbows and the corners of sunhats which tantalised the edges of the landscape.

'No, Mum — that's not France. See, all the umbrellas. Yes, it says Italy, Daddy and you. France must have been another time.'

When he was small, Danny would tease her lapses, although later, in thin-skinned adolescence, he shied away from the photos, especially the record of his own babyhood. He has outgrown all that again: last year, when his girlfriend Miranda was shown the albums, he smiled patiently as she laughed at his naked infancy hiding in foreign sand or at his tiny fingers clutching the wrist of an outsized Mickey Mouse.

I suppose that I first got the idea of organising the photos from the album which Maeve had brought with her to our marriage. After we returned from our honeymoon, during that first winter together, I had been avid for details of her past, the tiniest occurrence which would explain this new being I lived with. As she sat on my knee, crushing me into the one armchair which we then possessed, I gazed on the jumbled portfolio of her youth, where black and white First Communion and Confirmation portraits clustered around our full colour engagement picture; either side stretched innumerable rainy seaside Sundays and generations of pet dogs. Some of the leaves were so crowded that the photos overlapped untidily, while on the very next page the layout of alternate rectangular and square prints left irritating white spaces.

Yet, dismayed at the chaos though I was, I looked at them for weeks, touching my fingers to Maeve's wrist to slow her dream-like turning of the pages, asking yet again the names of cloudy relatives and classmates positioned in careful dissymmetry.

Really, I suppose I must have learned more about Maeve from the album as object rather than from the nature of its contents, since the litany of names and dates which she so uncharacteristically remembered without faltering was merely an unheeded soundtrack to my fascinated viewing. Only one part of the album bored me: the last part and the most recent chronologically. It was the small group of photos, for once homogeneous by the whim of their arranger, ending the album and terminating Maeve's spinster existence. Sparkling pastel dresses and the pervasive sky represented her first foreign trip, a fortnight's holiday with the girls from the office, an event for which they had saved each pay-day.

I suppose that in the early days of our marriage the memory had still rankled: it was only a couple of years old. I had asked her not to go, although we were not yet formally engaged, and she had gone anyway.

'I can't let the others down,' she had said as we sat in the pub, just before 'Last orders, please', rang out from the bar, silencing me. After some consideration, I decided on compliance, so I waved her plane off with a smile and asked the right questions when she returned.

Soon, I lost interest in Maeve's pre-history. As time passed, our son was born and the weight of our life together rolled us onward ever more quickly. Her old album was put away and left untouched after Danny's birth merited a new sort of pictorial record-keeping. Since our son became an adult, we have taken to opening these baby albums more often, straining to relate the images of emerging features and miniature limbs to the stranger who until recently greeted us each morning and evening at the bathroom door or faced us across the kitchen table. For the past couple of months, it has almost been a relief to relax our gaze and consider only our own wishes when planning our meals, our holidays, our life.

When I arrived home that night, armed with brochures and planned destinations, Maeve seemed subdued, telling me something about a stray cat; she always had a soft spot for hard luck cases. She seemed to accept my suggestions willingly enough and on the following Monday I hurried back at my lunch hour to the travel agent, my cheque already made out for the deposit.

I had approached Anna before the others arrived, to make sure that she had not decided this year to switch from her traditional block-booking of August on the leave roster.

'No problem,' she said as I told her of my plans, 'I'll be heading off in August as usual .... I suppose Sheila and Padraic can go early or late. Sheila said something about Spain in September.'

I knew there was a small family farm and an older brother awaiting her, but I asked politely, 'Any plans yourself?'

'No, no — just the usual.'

I returned to my desk, unworried about the others. I was the most senior, after all, and I always got first choice — after the section head, of course. Soon, very soon, Anna would move on with her bundles of files to the next floor with its airy offices which held only a single desk and heavily cushioned chair. I had heard the rumours in the corridors as I delivered my reports and I smiled as my informants leaned closer towards me with murmurs of consequential promotions and hinted congratulations. Once, when Anna was on holiday and the others had clattered out to lunch, I shut the door and sat for an hour in the chair beneath the window, testing its resilience, my hand on the phone to confound the suspicions of any sudden visitors.

Summer was the time for movement, when the brightness showed up the dust trails in corners from which filing cabinets had been shifted, and the bare spaces on walls gleamed in the red light of evening. Before I went on holiday this year, I decided, I would clear out the trays and the drawers of my desk with particular thoroughness.

II

That evening in February, when he came hurrying into the hall late from work, he was rustling with the news, unable to keep silent until he had his coat off.

'Maeve — wait till you see what I've brought home ....'

I heard the noise of his presence subside as he listened to find out which room I was in. But I did not answer him, knowing that he would find me soon enough. The newspaper creaked too loudly between my hands as I began the fire.

In the late afternoon I had dozed on the sofa underneath a rug, and now the draught made me shiver as the door burst open. He stood over me, smoky with the odour of his bus trip. I sat back on my heels and searched for the matches.

'There you are, working away. Hello, darling.'

'Hello. Had a busy day?'

While he began to narrate, I struck the first match and touched the small flame to the already unravelling paper. As it combusted, it shook soft flowers of ash onto the grate.

'You'll need more than that, Maeve. What about a few fire-lighters? Here, let me ....'

'I don't think there are any.'

He had moved towards the fireplace, but now stepped back again. I watched the grate in triumph as the papers caught and flared into sharp tongues of flame. Before the curling shards of ash could choke the fire's spread upward to the pyramid of turf and coal, I stood and edged him backward to the hall.

'It's quite cool in here. Come into the kitchen and I'll do the dinner while you tell me about your day.'

As he hung his coat under the stairs I saw him remove an oblong bundle and trail after me to the wide, brown-covered armchair we have had since our marriage. After lunch, I often sit there. He thinks it is his chair, but he has possession of it only after hours: before the evening meal and sometimes at weekends. It is mine the rest of the time, all the long days. I sit there a lot, reading or knitting as I listen to the radio, especially in the winter when it scarcely seems worth the effort to lock the doors and go out into the brief twilight which drifts through the streets between mid morning and early evening.

That particular day, when he was untypically late home, had already become unusual by breakfast time. When I had risen from bed and quickly descended the stairs, there were no familiar shapes hiding a pattern on the hall carpet, no envelopes beneath the letterbox.

'No bills today, at any rate.'

Sensing my disappointment, he had joked his way through cereal and toast, occasionally lapsing into introspection as he fingered his tie to check the knot before he raised his cup to his lips.

When he left, I toyed as usual with the machines which lined one wall of my kitchen. He has arranged them so that they all fit snugly underneath the worktop, each within easy reach of a socket, even with their flexes secured to the wall so that there can be no entanglements or extraneous shifting of plugs to incorrect power points. After I had dealt with the washing machine, the dishwasher and the tumble dryer, my triplets of steel perfection, it was lunchtime. The pips for the news sounded on the radio as I opened the fridge door and gazed on the array of cold food, choosing my lunch ingredients from among the cheeses and the savoury spreads.

When I had finished eating and cleared the table of crumbs and waxy fragments of cheese skin, the news was over and I turned off the transistor, quenching the miscellaneous chat and unidentifiable music. Already the brief daylight was fading behind the venetian blinds. I sat on in my part-time armchair and listened to the faint shuffle past of the nameless hours.

Since Danny had gone, the weeks had seemed to fuse into months, even into seasons. I found myself staring at my chequebook in the supermarket, trying to remember what numbers and words I had to inscribe on the dateline. Or, when he remained downstairs watching television, flung back into the sofa until well after the usual time, I would watch in vain for the signal for bed, forgetting that it was the weekend and we did not need to rise early the next day.

This flexibility in the temporal order did not perturb me. Rather it soothed my grief and made the initial waiting for Danny's step in the hall less onerous. Only, sometimes, the dislocation whenever I had to accommodate myself to the world's timetable, the strain of gathering my thoughts and forcing them into neat bundles, made me reach for the small phial which I got from the chemist.

When I told him of my problems, the doctor said it was all to do with the menopause. To allay my fears, he used the popular expression. 'It's just the Change,' he said, emphasising the capital letter. I knew that his diagnosis was wrong, although the expression captured perfectly my state of mind. 'Doth suffer a sea change,' I say to myself as I slide through the green water twice a week, alone in the municipal pool in the lull after lunchtime. As I push myself away from the ladder, the pool's surface divides and ripples beneath my chin, more effective than any prescribed pills, and I can almost accept the possibility that Danny will never return. The calming effect of that soapy, lukewarm liquid wrenches me from the armchair's embrace each evening and all the weekend, while he is watching, fuelling me with the energy to move around the house in a masque of busyness.

On that Friday, softened and moulded into my chair by the warmth of the gas fire, I had almost lost hold of hope and grief, and time again flowed past me unobtrusively. Then, in the mid-afternoon silence, I heard it, the click I had subconsciously been waiting for, the soft sigh following it which called my life back into focus. As the postman's steps receded down the gravel from the front door, I stood up slowly and went into the hall.

There were three items on the carpet, all of them face down: one white card and beneath it two brown envelopes angled across each other. When I had bent to pick them up, then weighed them carefully in my hand, I flipped over the card, identified the view and placed it in my apron pocket for later. Next, I studied the neatly pasted flaps of the manilla nine-by-fours, touching the edges with my finger-tips. This was always the best part, the greatest pleasure lying in an overestimation of the unknown contents.

Eventually I turned over the lighter envelope and recognised the cellophane window and printed postage frank of one or other of the regular bills. This was his domain and I quickly laid it down behind me on the hall table, unable to wait any longer for the other envelope's secret. I slit open the top jaggedly with my nails.

'Thank you for your competition entry. We are pleased to tell you that you have won a runner's up prize, which is being posted to you under separate cover ....'

I tugged at the hall door, but the mat was bare of any parcel; as I raised my eyes, coughing at the inrush of cold air, I saw a woman staring as she pulled her dog away from the gate. He staggered, his half-raised hind leg affecting his balance. She did not smile or speak and I did not recognise her face: lately, such a lot of the houses on this road have changed hands.

I brought my letter into the sittingroom, where my latest competition entries, ready for posting since morning, lay stampless on the mantelpiece. Now I stuffed them into the outside pocket of my handbag, deciding that I would, after all, leave my machinery and my armchair for a short while.

'Could I have three stamps, please, Mr Flynn?'

'You're just in time, today. Only ten minutes to go.'

Despite his own words, the postmaster refused to be hurried, tilting his head back to gaze through his bifocals at the addresses on my envelopes, then flicking solemnly through sheets of stamps of the wrong denomination until he paused and tore through the perforations.

'That'll be, let's see, eighty-four pence altogether.'

'Mr Flynn, was there any parcel, or a package perhaps, left here for me?'

'A parcel? Today? Don't remember any — the postman would have taken it for delivery, at any rate.' Glancing again at my envelopes, he stared through the grille with interest.

'Expecting something, were you? One of your competitions turn up lucky?'

I smiled evasively and stepped back to let the man behind me present his pension book, waiting until the postmaster's attention had transferred itself elsewhere. Then I looked over his head into the pigeon holes at the back of the room, searching among the bundles of forms for an extraneous shape: these things are so often overlooked in an apparently efficient place such as the post office, but they will never admit anything by rechecking in front of you.

While the man in front crouched down to the hole in the grille, watching his notes and coins being assembled and recounted, I continued to scan the heaps of unfranked letters and packets awaiting dispatch. As the man stepped away and I was once more face to face with the postmaster, I could not ask again, desperate as I was to receive my prize. Instead, I wet my stamps on the fraying sponge in its tin on the counter and slapped each into position with the palm of my hand.

The disc on the post-box outside was set to 'C': at five minutes before the collection hour, I was still in plenty of time. The envelopes slipped blissfully from the tips of my fingers through the slot and out of sight, and I heard them landing together on the pile of letters already posted.

As I stepped quickly away to the corner, something prompted me to turn for a last look back, and I saw the post van dodging in to the curb out of the line of traffic. I shivered in relief. Another few seconds and my envelopes would have struck smartly against clanging metal; there they would wait forlorn for the dangerous night collection, whose contents, as I knew from experience, were liable to loss and delay. No matter what the postman said, I knew about the bleary gaze of fumbling sorters forced into activity during unnatural hours.

The paper shop was crowded with children fighting to peer into the glass case full of penny bars and unwrapped, noxious-coloured chewing gum. I had to lean over them to pull the evening paper from its pile: beneath my arm, towers of coins were being exchanged for the sparse contents of brown paper bags.

As I strolled past the neighbours' houses, thick dusk, blown by the springing breeze, muffled my ears and blinkered my eyes. I was both cold and apprehensive as I glanced into the empty doorways next to my own: I usually avoided the out of doors world after dark, and it was difficult, without actually stepping into the shadowy gardens, to see if there was a parcel lying on the yellow tiles.

Then, for a moment, the breeze turned away and fled in the opposite direction. The haze lifted slightly and I saw, three porches down from mine, not an unbelonging, beckoning parcel but instead a small, tattered cat, a marmalade in better days. The auctioneer's sign near the gate had been there for weeks, weeds were well established at the flowerbed edgings and between the flagstones of the path, but this made no difference to the cat. Tail twitching, its gaze remained on the dusty glass of the hall door as I called to it softly, 'Puss, here, puss.' The house was so obviously dead: I envied the cat's faith.

I had almost forgotten my real errand, until I pushed shut my own door behind me and the empty hall echoed to the rumble of the letter-flap: then I realised that a whole post-less weekend stretched before me. There was no escaping the sense of loss for the rest of the evening, even after I had read my prize letter again before tucking it out of sight behind the books in the sittingroom.

'Any post this afternoon, dear?' he said as we moved from the kitchen after dinner. I indicated the bill on the hall table and he merely nodded at its shape, not interested in the rituals of anticipation and guesswork.

'Telephone, I suppose.'

'That reminds me,' I said as we sat down together on the sofa, 'there was a postcard as well, from Danny and Miranda, of course.'

'Well? How are they?'

As usual, he would never read the card himself. Children were still my responsibility, however diminished after twenty-five years. I looked at the blaze of colour on the mantelpiece, and obediently paraphrased the handful of scribble.

'They're fine. Miranda has a job at last. Danny's boss wants him to stay on for another six months. So ....'

He did not comment, or acknowledge the pain I had felt and which I now struggled to suppress, as I translated the words as a notice to quit home and childhood, leaving me — us — stranded together on the edge of the long sloping desert of middle and old age. Then he spoke, obviously of something important from the eagerness in his gestures, the flick of his elbow at my side. I looked at his lap and saw the reason for his preoccupation, the white domes of the Greek church floating upwards from the shiny page.

'Wait till you see these.'

Malta, even Cyprus: as I listened, I hoped it was what I would hear. But it wasn't, of course, it was that other country, that exact place in fact. Did he remember, or was he just unlucky? I still am not clear about these things, but I swear that I tried to resist it, this turn in our path which drew us towards it as we spun along, like the bad camber of a hurriedly finished motorway.

'Now that we'll be on our own this year — it could be a second honeymoon — after all, the first was a bit of a disaster.'

He laughed as he spoke, probably thinking of our wedding night when we sank fully clothed onto twin beds in the apartment building on the Italian Riviera. We had been unable to keep awake long enough to unpack our night clothes from the suitcases, let alone to consummate the past fortnight of dazed preparation. I had quite liked that Italian apartment, with its small balcony overlooking a residential block which cascaded geraniums, filling my head with a blaze of crimson and pink under the sunlight and my nostrils with a slightly peppery scent after dark as we waited to change for dinner.

'What about Italy, then?' I said. ' — or the Alps, perhaps? They were so beautiful.'

But he remained obdurate, his tone utterly reasonable.

'We've been to all those places before, you know. And as for the mountains — you remember, that was the time when Danny got sick in the car, and there was nowhere for miles.'

'Think of the views,' I said, or perhaps I just thought it.

'Think of all the driving', he said, flicking again through the pages alternately filled with black-clad peasant women and undressed North Europeans.

'I've been to Greece before.'

'Yes, dear, I remember. But we haven't, have we?'

After he had replaced the brochures carefully in his overcoat pocket, I lay in bed searching for a way out. I dozed, drifting away from him, but everywhere I turned he was there already, blocking any egress, gleefully waving in my face a bundle of tickets, repeating, 'And think of your swimming, dear, all that blue sea,' until I jerked awake in a prickly flush of panic. He lay beside me, quiet after his persuasions. Through a chink in the curtains, the edge of the city's glow threw slivers at my eyelids. The usual efforts to sleep were not working, my favourite image, water lapping under an opaque glass roof, shattered by his words. Then I heard an animal noise in a distant garden and wondered if the cat still clung to its doorway, loyal and starving.

A floorboard in the hall creaked in complicity as I moved from the kitchen with the bundle of scraps, holding it close to my layers of cardigan and overcoat. My slippers were efficiently quiet among the dark porches, but their thin soles did not protect my feet and I stepped slowly over the icy knives of the gravel. It was pitch dark in the porch of the empty house, but the cat was not there. I made sure by crouching and fumbling around each angle of the doorway, tensing to touch tattered fur or feel the razor slash of frightened claws.

In the end, I left the scraps there, tucked out of sight. When I went back the next day, even the paper was gone, but I never saw the cat again in the months before we left for Greece.

III

As the cabin began to level out, I loosened the webbing across my hips and stretched my legs as much as I could under the low seat in front. Maeve, I noticed, had completely unstrapped her own seatbelt, even though I had already pointed out to her the recommendations which were clearly set out in both words and pictures on the flight safety card.

It seemed only a matter of moments since the clouds had blotted out the fields and the sea, but when I glanced at my watch, I saw that more than twenty minutes had elapsed since take-off. By now, the section would be winding down from yet another busy week, pens clicking forgotten onto desks and paper shuffled less and less urgently, the torpor accelerated by the holiday month just beyond the horizon.

Over the past four days, I had disposed of all the outstanding items in my tray and made a spectacular clearance of my desk's contents. Yesterday, Anna had remarked on the rapid succession of memos passing under her signatory pen.

'Nothing like the prospect of a long break to shake off the cobwebs,' I had responded cheerfully as I dispatched the last of the cleared items and topped off the pile of large manilla envelopes in my out tray.

Now, as the plane floated towards the Channel, I knew that in the days of my absence from the organisation a legacy of neat pages would spread ripples along the adjacent corridors; their repercussions might, once or twice, even lift a mention of my existence upwards to the higher floors. Having steered in my prose a careful course between parsimony and excess, I did not fear that my name would be uttered in disapproving tones over the next two weeks; I was confident of pleasing in my absence, of tipping the balance in my favour, so that my cleared desk might never again have to be sullied by my particular presence, even that there might be another, higher office door ajar when next I stepped through the portals of the building.

My leavetaking of the section had been completely satisfying and the future was rich with unformulated promise, so that now as never before my work slipped from my thoughts, Anna and the others drifting greyly into their weekend lives and away from mine. In this temporary blankness, I turned to Maeve, silent in the window-seat.

'You remembered to disconnect the fridge, didn't you, dear? And the cooker?'

She remained looking out through the porthole, although as far as I could see there was nothing but dirty cotton-wool below and above, and when she answered me she directed her words at the wing of the plane. The house was technically her concern, but I wondered now if I should have rechecked doors and windows, notwithstanding the list I had left on the kitchen table.

'Yes, I did. And the washing machine, and the dishwasher. Everything has been... disconnected. You put it all in the list, didn't you?'

'Of course, dear. Of course.'

I was never sure if Maeve really read my lists. Now I knew. I reached out and touched the sleeve of a bright two-piece I had not seen before.

'Is that a new purchase, Maeve? It's very nice.'

The cabin crew were already steering their trolleys from opposite ends of the plane, to meet in the middle in plenty of time for the second trip with the food trays. Since we were seated over the wing near the central emergency exit, precisely as I had requested, it would be some time before the wobbling pyramid of cans and plastic bottles reached us, but I wanted to settle the matter.

'Feel like a drink, dear?'

'Oh, wine I think. Red, please.'

I was surprised, but did not remark on it. Maeve did not usually touch alcohol, preferring some strange mixture of mineral water and orange juice.

'Baptising the new outfit, eh?'

I began to dig in my pockets for change, anxious to reserve the notes in my wallet for the taxi ride home from the airport. Maeve must have felt the movement of my elbow in the narrow seat. She turned and held out some coins, about two pounds' worth.

'Here, pay for it with this. You might need your change later, for another one, maybe.'

Then she added, as I took the money, 'You don't mind if I have one, do you? It's just so claustrophobic in here....'

'Of course not, dear. You can drink whatever you want, you know that.'

Later, as I dozed, Maeve's fingers gripped my arm and I turned away from the aisle to see a dazzle of light on the clouds far below, and, above, a blue like that of the travel poster.

'Look, quickly, the Alps.'

By the time I had undone my seatbelt and leaned across her to the window, the opening in the clouds, if there had really been one, had been sucked away again.

'You just missed it. What a pity, they were so beautiful.'

'Yes. Well, never mind,' I said, 'shouldn't be too long now.'

But it was almost an hour later before the huge plane circled down over sea, then land, then tipped with a tiny impact onto the edge of the runway. Still studying the map of our flight-path, I was taken by surprise when the cabin crew jumped up and reached for their hats in the overhead racks. I craned with the rest for a first glimpse of foreign soil as the wheels rumbled slower and slower, but all I could see was a tiny structure half a mile away across the glittering tarmac. Then the plane stopped and the bumping of knees against the seats in front and the hauling down of hand luggage began.

As each passenger reached the top of the steps, there was a momentary delay while the stewardess offered a hand to shake and the eyes made the adjustment from dim lighting. I shivered, shaking off the now chilly temperature of the pressurised cabin. It was half past seven in the evening, local time, but the terminal building, only yards away now, still threw little shadow, and heat blasted my face as I struggled down from the belly of the plane.

At first, when we stepped into the arrivals lounge and discovered what seemed little more than a stifling shed, I thought there had been some mistake.

'Are you sure this is the right island?' I joked to one of the women beside me. There was no sign of any representative from the tour company and we waited at the single conveyor belt for whatever it might send, listening to the continuous baffling announcements and facing the indecipherable notices pasted to the walls. Maeve sat patiently beside the hand luggage, her face pink from exhaustion and wine, while I wandered in search of someone who spoke English. The heat had not lessened with the declining sun, and my clothes, so unsuitably light in the biting wind at home, now weighed down my shoulders and my back with patches of moisture.

After an hour, the suitcases arrived without warning and I leaped forward gratefully, barking my shins on the edge of the metal belt.

'Just wait till I get to a telephone,' I kept saying as we struggled out through the other door of the building and into the scarcely cooler oven of the car park. But even as I drew breath to repeat my sentiments, a courier in a freshly smelling uniform stepped forward from beneath the spreading, furzy trees and glanced down at the labels on our luggage.

'This way, please.'

When we had seated ourselves in the air-conditioned bus, I felt the cool jets from the ceiling playing on my throbbing face.

'Look at them,' I said to Maeve, pointing out the knots of people here and there about the concrete, still wincing in full sun, still without leadership.

'Independent travellers. Flight only,' said the man in the seat in front, turning around, and we chuckled together for a moment.

When at last the bus was full, the courier entered and picked up her microphone. She nodded to the driver and the coach began to rotate slowly in the narrow car park, reviving uneasy memories of the take-off and landing we had recently survived. Then, we accelerated out onto a surprisingly smooth road scattered with the outlying debris of a large town. I consulted the crude map which the courier had just handed out, but the scale was too small for me to establish with any certainty our actual position.

'Would that be the main town?' I asked Maeve, but she just shrugged and smiled vaguely, then picked up the map and put it down again.

After only a minute or two, we reached the first of the apartment blocks with a claim on our particular group. At each stop, as the departure of families and young girls reduced the bus load stage by stage to a handful, I felt my anticipation sweeten. With each mile of road the conglomeration near the airport was further away: my careful perusal of the brochures in February had paid off, we would be staying as far away as possible from the frantic town and the concrete squalor of its surrounding villages.

Soon the bus turned off onto a secondary road lined by pine-like trees and occasional small villas and we began to point out to each other the far-off glittering windows across the valley which swam though the blue twilight. I think it was then that I realised it, just then, as I surprised myself by giving Maeve's arm a squeeze and the driver made a wide turn into the forecourt of the small hotel.

We were alone together for the first time, my mind wiped clean of the organisation and its struggles, Maeve untrammelled by the demands of a toddler or the fads of an adolescent. In the dusk, the white building was very like the Venetian *pensione* where we had honeymooned, but this time we were without post-wedding exhaustion. Strangely, watching Maeve jump down from the steps of the bus in her bright skirt, all the years in between seemed never to have existed.

After the long trip, the tiled floors and the lofty alcoves in the hotel lobby were refreshing and the fast dance music booming from the empty bar was cheerful. As we queued at the desk, Maeve pressed her hands to her ears. But, when I looked at her enquiringly, fearing that she was already retreating behind old barricades, she smiled quickly.

'It's just the trip. I'm fine now that we're here at last ....'

'Just arrived today, have you?'

A tall man with gleaming teeth leaned on the other end of the counter with the assurance of a week's suntan. I might have aspired to his beige shirt with its epaulets and turn-ups on the sleeves, but I would never have dared to wear the khaki shorts — I know my limitations.

'That's right,' I said. 'And how's the weather been this week?'

I did not like him, perhaps because the overall military effect of the clothing jarred with his casually hairy limbs, or maybe because of the way his eyes raked Maeve's figure from time to time. In answer to my question he laughed heartily, showing off his teeth, but whatever words he was about to utter were swallowed up in the bustling return of the hotel proprietor and the red tape of arrival.

When at last we climbed the two flights of stairs, the bedroom, like the rest of the hotel, was high-ceilinged, but oppressive after the day's heat, until Maeve pulled up the shutters and slid back the terrace window to let the cooler draught in and herself out.

'What did you think of Adonis down there?' I raised my voice as little as possible to reach her on the balcony, thinking that he might be somewhere in earshot still.

'Who? The proprietor?'

'No — you know, the Englishman.'

'Oh, him.' Maeve laughed. 'Fine set of teeth, hasn't he? Wonder where he bought them.'

Apparently, it had not occurred to her, or perhaps she didn't care, that her voice might carry downwards in the quiet air. It was about then, as I heaved my suitcase onto the bed nearest the window and began to fit the key into the lock, that my eye was caught by the moving black thread on the tiled floor between the bathroom and the balcony.

'Maeve, come here, look at this.'

She seemed to take a long time to respond, and when at last the curtain was pushed aside, she scarcely glanced at the straight line leading from between her feet inwards under my bed.

'Oh, it's just the ants, they were everywhere, I remember. We'll get something for them tomorrow, a spray or a smoke coil.' Then she saw my disgust and laughed.

'Come on out on the balcony before it's completely dark. The view is wonderful. Leave the unpacking till later.'

I was still worried as I stepped out into the open air.

'Were they actually in your apartment?'

'Of course. But we were never there, so it didn't really matter.'

She laughed again, so that I had to smile at last, trying to put out of my mind the thought of stumbling barefoot to the bathroom in the dark, and beneath that something more disquieting still, all the more so for being only half-sensed. It was as if I knew that turning my head fully round I might see a large spider on her bare arm inches from my face.

As we undressed later, I felt the need to embrace her surprisingly supple body; but she climbed with a sigh into her narrow bed and switched off the lamp so quickly that I did not disturb her. Maeve has always been so obliging about these things, and there were, after all, thirteen nights of our holiday remaining.

The next morning, the air was refreshing when I opened the balcony door, the sun not yet round our corner of the building, and the shadows of trees hung deep and cool. But only an hour later, as we finished breakfast, the thermometer was rising rapidly and the sunlight reached between the blinds to strike our bare arms on the table.

I was gritty with lack of sleep, my bones aching from the strange bed and the first insect bites irritating my skin. Yet, as we sat over the crumbs of the meal, I intended to keep to the plan I had formulated among my damp sheets: the town for souvenirs, the temple nearby, perhaps the historical light show in the evening.

'The temple,' said Maeve, 'isn't that a long way away?'

'It's quite near the town, according to this book. "The Temple at Kardaki", it says, "three stars." There isn't anything else with that many ....' I flicked through the pages rapidly. 'No — sorry, there is a monastery with the same rating. But that's miles away, on the far coast.'

'It might be more interesting, though,' she said, her voice more distinct as she lowered her cup to its saucer. 'The temple is only — I mean, it's probably only a heap of stones by now.'

But I showed her the paragraph in the book, and stressed the importance of assimilating the culture of a place, now that we were free of Danny's adolescent foibles. She could not find any counter-argument, and nodded her head.

'There'll be plenty of time for swimming tomorrow,' I said, clinching it.

Later, I was sorry that I had been so enthusiastic. As the guidebook had warned, there was a steep climb down to the Kardaki spring below the ruined temple. As we descended, my legs trembled a little, tired from the morning's sightseeing in the old quarter and the detour to the museum. I had not wanted to visit the neglected galleries which did not merit a single star in my guide, but Maeve insisted it was on the way to the temple, and that there was a particular sculpture worth seeing. Afterwards, I tried not to think of that Medusa in pride of place on the ground floor: unlike Perseus, I was given no shield to mirror the monster's frozen hair of whirling snakes and blank eyes, merely glimpsing a brief reflection in the lenses of Maeve's sunglasses as I turned away.

'Let's go,' I said, 'we've seen it now.'

'Just a minute.'

She walked past me to the plinth. I heard her breathing as she stood there, until I couldn't bear the wordless heat any longer and stepped down the curving stairs into the portico, where the sun struck my feet and pinioned them to the marble. Even here, the statue's gaze seemed to writhe outwards from the plinth and fasten itself onto the back of my neck, and I jumped slightly when Maeve suddenly reappeared, thrusting forward her latest souvenir for my inspection.

'You're not going to send that to anyone, are you?'

I glanced away from the card's stark impression of the statue. She had removed her sunglasses and her eyes smiled teasingly.

'I thought Danny might like it. Danny and Miranda.'

'No,' I said, 'I don't think so.'

She blinked at the card and put it away in her bag, then walked ahead of me to the pavement, turning right towards the old harbour. I did not follow at first, struggling to pull the crumpled guidebook from my hip pocket.

'Just a second, I have the book here ... we could take a short-cut through the town. It's getting very warm.'

'Yes, it's still very hot. I'll give you my hat. This is the right way, around the old harbour to the temple. We must keep to the route.'

I put the guidebook away, hiding myself under the straw hat. There were blue signs at the turnings and she followed them, unhesitating, ignoring my need to pause, to shake off the burning on my head, to recover from what I had seen in the museum. Although, in retrospect, it was more what Maeve had seen and I had not which was worrying. At an old church, I hung back in the shade, lifting my hat to wipe the band of wetness under my hairline, until she sensed I was not following and turned in the middle of the white road to wait for me.

'Mind the car!'

She heard me and reacted, stepping into the margin and sheltering her face from the cloud of dust which sprayed from the wheels. The driver was laughing at me as he passed, his companions bobbing up and down in the back seat.

'Bastards!' I shouted, but the effort was too great and my breath tore at the back of my throat.

We trudged onwards, leaving the road for the signposted footpath. As we turned off, the villagers sat and watched us from the shade, gaunt men with heavy working shirts and, among them, a priest in a tall hat and starched black robe.

On the precipitous stony descent that might once have been steps, something jumped from between my feet and I almost fell, lurching against her shoulder. She did not falter, but guided me down the rest of the way, until we came to a crumbling, stone lion and a trickle of water.

I stood in the shade of tall shrubs. She knelt beside the water on the rocky grass, her bag tossed to one side.

'Careful,' I said, my voice whispering through the dryness of my throat. 'There could be snakes, or scorpions.'

'Not here,' she said and she drank, cupping her hands close to her bended face, again and again. Then she stood.

'Now, your turn.'

The water was surprisingly tasteless, unrefreshing despite its cool slither past the roof of my mouth. After I had drunk a few times, I splashed it on my face. As I moved back, feeling the droplets already vanishing into the puffiness of my skin, she bent and drank again, then cupped the water and raised her hands above her upturned face.

'Is that it? A Venetian fountain?' I had felt her draw away as I drank and wondered if she shared my sudden disappointment at the place.

'Oh, no. Long before that.' Now she did not seem disappointed, but rather sated; her voice was just above a murmur, and the water shone in the light as it sprayed out from her fingers onto her face and her hair.

'This is the spring which rises up there, in the temple of Kardaki ... her temple.'

'Whose temple?'

But she merely laughed, and in that laugh I felt myself step backward out of the shade and into the unabating sun; while she seemed rooted to the spot, frozen with water dripping down her arms.

'Come on, Maeve, it's too hot here.' I was trying to find the exit from the overgrown grove. I turned and turned until dizziness made me stop. Then she stood and stepped out of the clearing through a gap which I had not seen.

Afterwards, I tried to ascribe my queasiness to the heat and not to the suspicion which I dared not voice and swallowed instead. She did not really seem any different, not yet, but she remained distracted during the sound and light show, perking up only when the rumbling bus had deposited us back at the village below the hotel and the smell of food wafted from the tavernas lined up along the road.

All the loudspeakers were playing the same music, a sort of disco bazooki beat, as far as I can tell about these things. The least noisy was also the most crowded, but we found a table near the kitchen.

'Oh, swordfish — and moussaka, of course. What are you going to have?'

I smiled wanly at Maeve's enthusiasm, my taste-buds failing to respond to the smell of charcoal and grilling meat which thickened the warm night air.

'Just a salad, perhaps, if they have it.'

'Not hungry?'

'It's probably the heat, and the change. I'd better stick with something light this evening. No point in risking an upset, is there?'

After we had given our order and as we waited for the food, for hours, it seemed, I looked around at the other diners. Most of the women wore dresses slightly too young for them, suntan or no suntan, and the men all reminded me of the brown-skinned brute we had already encountered in the hotel. I could see their eyes sliding from their platefuls to where we sat, weighing up Maeve as if she were some newly arrived brood mare.

At a nearby table, I watched a crowd laugh excessively at something the bronzed man in the khaki had just said.

'Oh, Harry, you're priceless.' One of the women leaned forward as she tittered, as if to expose even more of her décolletage.

The waiter presented our meals with a flourish and departed.

'The fish is lovely, you should have had some. Want a taste?'

'No thanks,' I said. Then I leaned forward and the fried smell of her food made my stomach heave a little.

'What a crowd of idiots, eh?'

She followed the slight movement of my head and looked sideways at the other tables, as if she had not yet noticed their clamour, although she could scarcely have been unaware of the barrage of glances aimed in her direction ever since we had arrived.

'They look quite normal to me, the usual sort of tourists. Go on, try just a little of this. I promise you'll like it.'

'No, thanks.'

At least the wine was good and as the evening passed I felt myself gradually unwinding, my nausea fading with the smell of burnt oil from the kitchen.

We were almost the last customers to leave the taverna. Beyond the village, the road was so black that we had some difficulty finding our side turning. But we had walked only a few yards up the track when I heard the music blaring from the hotel, across the courtyard and through the imposing iron gates.

'I hope they turn that thing down later on,' Maeve said. 'I might have considered a last drink if the bar was quieter.'

My legs dragged along the gravel and my head rolled a little. I had been dreading any suggestion of a nightcap and now, it seemed, the music had saved me. My spirits rose at the thought of a soft pillow and cool sheets.

'At least we'll always be able to find the hotel,' I said.

'It's not darkest Africa, you know.' She chuckled in the darkness and I thought again of the insect life which had chosen our room for its locus vivendi, the millions nestling into inconceivably small spaces behind the insolently smooth walls.

'Of course,' I said, 'you've seen it all before, haven't you?'

IV

On the first morning of the holiday, he insisted on travelling as far as the town. We had skirted it the evening before, but I remembered little of that arrival, or of the long flight down over the Alps and on to the fringe of islands off the south-west coast. I was too apprehensive, wondering how soon I would give everything away, yet unable to recall what it was I had to hide. After he had left his seat and gone to the washroom, a couple across the aisle tried to strike up a conversation. I did not resist very strongly, even welcoming the distraction. They were youngish, unburdened by their children, gradually becoming tipsy on gins and tonic.

'We left them with Mary's folks. They're too small to bring on holiday.'

'What ages are they?' I was afraid to stare any more at the shapeless cloud formations, and there was nowhere else to look except down the long, narrow aisle to where the senior stewardess plucked open cabinets and unloaded endless cellophane-wrapped trays.

'Let's see, Stephen is four and Samantha's six.'

'Six and a half.'

The woman looked up sharply from her inflight magazine and I felt she was less pleased than her husband about leaving the children behind. I thought of the pleasure of Danny's first swim in the Mediterranean, his brown skin naked beneath a white sunbonnet as he thrashed about in warm wrinkles of sea. At other times, the two of them would watch as I struck out into the depths, Danny shrieking as my head disappeared for a moment into the trough of a small wave.

The last sight I had of the couple was after we landed and I waited in the queue at the door of the plane.

'Fantastic,' the man was saying as he raised his face to the sky, almost tripping on the first metal step. Behind him, the woman, now wearing a red baseball cap, placed her feet more carefully as she followed. I kept my eyes on her ankles, afraid to look up and discover why I had not wanted to set foot in this place again. My shadow, deep black beneath the strong evening sunlight, moved steadily ahead of me down the steps.

But, as I jolted onto the tarmac and caught a glimpse of the single small hangar and the name on the terminal building, I could not recognise them, and such was my relief that I laughed aloud. He turned to look at me, then was distracted by the conversation of other passengers. Perhaps I had imagined it all, I thought, as we underwent the protracted formalities, perhaps I had never really been here all those years ago.

As I waited at the luggage conveyor belt, there was still nothing to jog my memory and I could not even picture the faces of Alison and Joanne, my friends and fellow-travellers from the long-ago office. I had lost touch with them even before the wedding, embroiled as I was in the details of house-buying and music for the organist; and later he had not exactly encouraged any renewal of those particular friendships. After all, we had each other, and a neat circle of mutual friends. Soon, we also had Danny.

Danny was not with us this time. For a moment, as he moved away from my elbow, there was the same burst of exhilaration as once before when I stepped onto unknown soil, but it struggled and died as I watched him search out the too-familiar trappings of bus, courier, fellow tourists. The lonely airport set in brown hills, the diffident customs officials, even our companions on the bus: all were the same as in other years.

I sat back into my padded seat as we listened to the standard welcome, not expecting now to be surprised into remembrance. I had seen many resorts in the years since my first foreign holiday and, whether in reality or in the small photographs heading my newspaper competitions, they were all alike. The stocky, dark men who guarded the bright umbrellas and faded deckchairs might have been brothers, and the beach was always the same, different only in the colours of its warning flags.

Then, as the bus left behind the usual concrete apartments, I could only stare through the window in bewilderment and join the others in their gasps of surprise at the rolling green hills and valleys, the whiteness of the flat-roofed houses. Amazement briefly unlocked the past, but I could remember only blurred images fading into greyness at the corners, shapes which could have been a multi-story hotel and neon-lit bars lining a dusty route to the beach. In that landscape, there were none of the trees which the bus now shouldered aside in casual brutality: perhaps there had been none, or perhaps I had just not noticed.

'No,' I said in reply to his query, 'no, it wasn't like this where I stayed the last time, it must have been in some other part of the island.'

I did really want to tell him, to throw myself utterly on his mercy in the midst of this uncharted land, but the innermost door of my mind had shut itself again. When we reached it, I could not even see in the ornate plaster-work of the hotel the Italian reminders he insisted on. In fact, I could discover no similarity whatsoever to any place I had visited before.

'Well, the surroundings are different, I suppose,' was all he said, smiling and confident at the veracity of his own judgement. His spirits were still high the next morning while he planned our trip to the old town.

'Before it gets too hot,' he announced as we stood up from the first breakfast of the fortnight, 'we can get the shopping out of the way and then forget all about it.'

He had raised his voice, trying I suppose to shame the others in the diningroom into following, but his audience, already clad in bikinis and shorts for the beach, merely looked impressed.

While he went upstairs for his lists, separate ones as usual for postcards and for souvenirs, I wandered out into the garden at the back of the hotel, to where a swimming-pool glistened with leaves torn free by the night's wind. The temperature was already high enough for me to long for the somnolent blue water and the polished tiles beneath. Breakfast in the hotel was still in progress and, for a while, no-one stepped outside the building or appeared at the balcony windows. Unwatched, I could take off my sandals and sit on the warm stone parapet with my feet just touching the cool wetness.

After what seemed only moments, I heard him come in search of me, crunching along the gravel path.

'There you are. What are you doing?'

'I thought you'd be longer. It's so warm and the water looked lovely ....'

While I refastened the thongs over my slippery feet he threw a twig, breaking the surface of the pool.

'Better than the public baths, isn't it?' he was saying. 'Wonder if they disinfect this one, though?'

The town bus stopped every few yards, yet for me the road to civilisation was too short. My side of the coach faced the unchanging beach; the interior of the island slid past the opposite windows before I could begin to see it in the small spaces between the elbows and waists of the swaying commuters. As I leaned further out, the passengers changed their positions, and immediately I recognised a middle-aged woman without a wedding ring in the seat beyond the aisle. I sat back, pretending I hadn't seen her, but he too had noticed. He leaned forward and looked into her face.

'Hello — very hot, isn't it? You were on the coach last night, weren't you?'

'Yes,' she said, turning and bobbing her head to us, 'I think, in fact, we're in the same hotel as you — myself and my sister, that is. How do you do?'

'This is Maeve,' he said, gesturing at my seat, 'and I'm Tom.'

'Glad to meet you. Millicent Clancy.'

A shuffle forward to the door cut her off from us for a moment. He took advantage of the pause.

'What did she say her name was?' His breath tickled my ear hotly. I hoped it might end at that, but he leaned out again unselfconsciously as soon as the thinning crowd allowed further communication.

'That's an unusual name you have — if you don't mind me saying so.'

She smiled freely at him, not seeming to notice the taut muscles of my face. Normally, I did not bother about these things, but something about her drew my interest. After all, she was the age I would be in another ten or fifteen years.

'Yes, all of us were called something like that, something old-fashioned, you might say. My father's idea, I believe. My sisters, poor things, were really unlucky — .'

I tried to interrupt her confession, to let her know that she did not have to submit to his interrogation: she was not me, after all, and middle-age was hers to enjoy in peace.

'You're lucky to have sisters,' I said, 'I was an only child.'

'Only, but not lonely, isn't that right, Maeve?' he said, linking his arm through mine, then drawing breath for another question. But, before he could do so, she gave him what he wanted, gracefully.

'I'm glad that Letty, Ginnie and I are so close, more like friends than sisters, I suppose. We nearly always take our holiday together, but this time Ginnie had to stay at home. She's not too well at the moment ....'

With her last words, her voice had dropped, as if she spoke to herself. I was disturbed, sensing her pain. Beside me he had his hand up to his face, and I thought I could feel his silent laughter against my ribs. I nudged him sharply, then wondered if I was wrong always to expect the worst of him, as he spoke into the lull of conversation on the bus.

'Are you on your own, today? If you'd like company, you're welcome to come with us — .'

'Thank you, you're very kind. But I'm not going right into town, just as far as the post office, to ring Ginnie. And then I have to get back — Letty will be waiting for me at the hotel. But, thank you.'

'Well, if there's anything we can do, Millicent ....'

He was at his most expansive, but I hoped that she would not subject herself to a session of our company, my concern as much for myself as for her. I did not want my darkest feelings thrown into relief by the presence of a stranger.

'Do call me Milly — it's less formal.'

She smiled again at us as she left the bus.

'Bit of a fruitcake, old Milly, eh?'

Bored, then, he took out the map from the courier's information pack and spread it across our knees. The scale showed the town as a compact grid, its old central streets a web in one corner. In reality, as the bus circled the endless one-way thoroughfares filled with noisily combatant cars and pedestrians, there seemed to be no end to it all. It was too large and bustling a place for a small island, and the green countryside was invisible from its centre. But somewhere on the far side, beyond the jumble of high-rise offices and sleazy apartments, lay the quiet villages and small hills of the interior. Among them was Kardaki.

He had pinpointed the site of the temple and its spring that morning, just as he had happened on the island on a February night when his usual bus had gone; he had been led onward through the pages of the brochure, and now the guidebook, by unerring chance. As soon as he spoke the name of the temple, a warning bell rang in my thoughts, but I could not dissuade him from his reasonable arguments.

'We'll visit the old town first,' he said, 'and then it's just a couple of hundred yards past the harbour to the beginning of the track. There'll be plenty of time to take photographs and get back to the fort for the pageant in the evening.'

'It's a lot to take on in this climate,' I said, but he was firm.

'We can rest in the shade any time you want to, Maeve.'

As we left the bus, the sun poured its sticky heat over my head and down my body. I noticed that wetness was already spreading across the back of his new white shirt, but he refused to slow down, marching ahead of me to the old quarter, so that I almost ran to keep up with him. For I did not want to lose him, not today.

Even before we reached the smelly maze of ancient alleys and squares which had tucked itself into the town's armpit, I could feel the panic bubbling up in my throat, my eyes and ears seared by the light reflecting off the cars and shop windows. At times, the crowd intruded a little of itself between us, so that I almost lost sight of his bobbing head. At each crossing, cars hooted and jammed themselves into the throng of shoppers to make progress, and try as I might I could not avoid the abuse of drivers and pedestrians alike.

Above everything else, the language confounded me: when babbled in my ear by a passing hawker it was strange enough, but the street-signs and shopfronts flickered writing at me from all sides that might have been part of a cypher. In its oddly familiar angles and curves, the ancient alphabet spoke to me of the past, but I did not wish to receive the message; I did not want to have to remember.

Had I been alone, I would have turned back at that point and fled through the streets outwards to where the town's tendrils lost themselves in the hills. I might even have sought out Milly. Of course, had I been truly alone and free to choose, I would never have come back to the island. All during the slow spring and wet summer of home, I had not wanted to return, and my apprehension was redoubled as I stepped behind him into the first of the cobbled streets which wound out of sight into the mid-morning.

From the moment we turned that first corner, I no longer knew the way back, I made a lunge forward and caught at his arm, I trod on his heels, averting my face from the perpendicular walls, while he sought out churches and souvenir shops. Everywhere we went, the crowd jostled past us or spoke over our heads, as if we were souls so lost as to be beyond saving.

It was hot enough now to be a sort of hell, reducing even his enthusiasm to silence. It was after noon, and all the stern women and laughing men had vanished from their stalls and dim shops. The singing birds too had fallen silent and their cages swung emptily beside shuttered windows. I realised that I was completely dependent on his guidance, that this place was a maze from which I might never escape. When I said that, he laughed and told me that the labyrinth and its monster were the property of a different island. Then he stopped suddenly at a junction of identical paths, and my heart froze.

'Umm ... this way, I think.'

'Are you sure?'

'Well, that's what the map says, isn't it?'

We had nowhere to go but on, deeper between the crouching houses, averting our eyes from the sunlight knifing over the edge of the tiles.

'But we've been along here before — it was only a minute ago,' I said, fighting off the desire to let myself fall down onto the boiling, greasy pavement. My feet dragged behind his along the deserted streets and down the stinking stairways to further silent squares.

Just as I felt my knees buckle and blackness edge my vision, a breath of dead fish and tar teased my nostrils. We had reached the harbour at the edge of the town and I stepped with delight from malodorous shade, welcoming the shards of sun which burned my arms and my insteps. Even he was not himself, agreeing without argument to let me sit in the waterside café under the chestnut trees while he entered the nearer streets once more in search of a last souvenir.

'I won't get lost this time,' he said.

'Perhaps,' I said, 'you should have packed a ball of twine, and then you could have given me one end to hold onto .... '

Beyond the edge of the promenade and the bustle of shipping stretched the flat blue sea as far as the horizon. While he dallied among the reopened shops up to the steep, dead-end steps, I was content below, viewing the boats and breathing the salt air, scanning the faces which disembarked from the white decks; at last I was bulwarked against my earlier terror. The promenade was roofed by groves of chestnut trees and striped café awnings and edged by heaving ferries, each with its queue of patient travellers; with a little effort I could have stood up from my seat and joined them in their transition from the old life to somewhere new.

In the spaces between ferries, I looked up at the buttressed fort which brooded over the town and the water. I knew that the pageant there was next on his itinerary. Later, after the trip to the spring, I was not sorry to leave the town behind and go with him to step over sad memories as we paced the ramparts, our feet soft on tussocks of sea grass as we followed the gaze seaward and homeward of the ghosts who still limped among the scattered battlements.

I stood above the harbour and listened to him read aloud of those hopeful battalions of sailors who came from far and wide to the island, whose long-voyaged ships broke at last against the stony coast, leaving those who could to scramble ashore in disarray.... After a while I did not really hear him. It seemed that the fortress was finally at rest, after generations of betrayal: I could see that the builders' work was already half undone. To demolish it all, the island and its seas had drawn only on the arsenal of time, softening stones and opening up stairwells without paying attention to the provenance of architecture.

As his voice faltered, I disengaged myself from the day-long struggle with the town, admitting a truce, and came back to evening again. We turned at some instruction from his book and there, across the ramparts, the mainland peaks melted into an ochre sky. I had not known we were so close to the heavy mass of the continent, but yet there was no substance to this land we faced. The shipping straits were too deep against the sheer coasts, too wide under our feet to admit of limitations; appropriating for commerce a slim path across the waves seemed merely another feeble gesture against the endless, anarchic sea.

Now, the sun was setting across the island behind us, sliding below the horizon into another hemisphere. I saw him looking northwest to where the final blaze of light was cut off by the mountains, and the higher, more jagged peaks were thrown into brief silhouette. Then he turned away quickly from the view and spoke.

'We'd better hurry if we're to catch the light show further along.'

As the *son et lumière* began and the music swelled and buildings on the waterfront were spotlit one by one, he tried to take my hand. I let him, although I was conscious of no communion in the meeting of our clammy flesh. The narration which died away from time to time beneath the chatter of children, only to rise again tinnily in the pauses, all the carefully arranged pyrotechnics: these were mere sound and light against the backdrop of the restless bay and its purple curtain. Somewhere out there, in daylight, the mainland might have been, no more real than the pageant. The shadows and murmurs of the crowd, and the swivelling spotlight which picked out convenient monuments, reminded me of the church into which we had stumbled on our frantic odyssey through the town.

'What did you think of Saint Spiridon's today?'

'Ssh.'

He leaned forward, away from me, refusing to remember his discomfiture when, having found our way at last to the site marked on his map, there was a service in progress. He had hurried out again, pretending that he could not read his guide-book in the dimness; but I guessed that the urgency of the chant and the head-dresses of the priests were too pagan, too untidy for him. Ignoring his beckoning hand, I sank down beside the heavily clad, veiled women. I sought only to rest my burning feet against the chill tiles, but when the chant began again I let it wash over me like the small artificial waves in my twice-weekly swimming pool. I felt under my bare toes the ancient foundations of the building and gazed around the walls at the niches which each contained a silverwork casket. Worn with age and the polishing of the faithful's fingertips, I guessed that they must hold the relics of the saint. Each separate limb or fragment of clothing had at the foot of its reliquary a bouquet of tiny, shivering flames.

I sat on, almost hypnotised by the play of light and shadow. But when he tired of his history and approached fumbling down the rows, he woke me from my vision. Then the bowed heads and folded hands of the people around me were too much like the obeisance I had long practised before my trinity of kitchen appliances, and my mood evaporated. I started up from my seat and steered him back to the lighted doorway.

'Take your time,' he hissed, glancing round then in apology at the bent heads.

I tried to tell him what had happened, but already he had set off again through the streets and I followed, losing the church after a single turning. It was too late then to explain convincingly how as I sat there the chant had suddenly died away and the foundations begun to crumble back into the moist black earth from which they had once risen.

In a pause of the show we looked past the heads of children to the deep water outside the harbour, and I hoped again that now was the time.

'Don't you think,' I began, 'that this is all very artificial. I mean — the town, the history books. There's no magic in any of it, not like it must really have been, when the legends were recent history ....'

I had lost my words again, but I knew from his tone that already I had said too much. If I was not careful, the pinprick of doubt I had glimpsed in his eyes at Kardaki, when, beyond caution, I had led the way to the fountain, would deepen and spread, engulfing me again.

'I find it all quite fascinating, myself.'

His tone was acerbic; his hand stiffened in mine, ready to draw away, the gesture to be put down to an unsuccessful experiment. I gripped his fingers more tightly.

'You have to admit that the town is quite frightening really, in a bullying kind of way. Isn't it? For instance when you — we — got lost today — .'

'We weren't lost. The map was wrong. Probably an old one.'

'So is the town.'

As the show started again, I shook off rancour and turned inwards, feeling the stirrings of something I could not name. It had come to me that the things I had held to myself as comfort down through the long years, Danny and the competitions with which I had replaced him, were as nothing compared with the real power whose source I could sense was somewhere on this island: my feelings of elation and terror were too strong for it not to be.

I laughed suddenly, thinking that if I told my doctor about it all, he would merely say that my hormones were out of order. Then I shivered, clenching his fingers again, willing him to answer my call. The past was coming back to me, the hidden places of the island beckoned to me with a force I could not resist. He had begun it, with his insistence on the island, the town, even the very spring.

'But you must have been here before — you know the way, don't you?' he said on the road back to the town. I could say nothing, dumb with too much knowledge of something I was only gradually remembering. When I followed the road out from the town, while I stepped surefootedly among the fragrant bushes to the fountain, it was as if I was following an unseen guide. The clearing itself was not empty when we arrived: shadows fluttered among the leaves and, as I drank, I could hear the rustle of voices behind the water trickling through my fingers, but I was afraid to look round.

Even as we had stepped off the plane, there had been a shape etched beneath my steps on the concrete that was not my silhouette; I could not know if he too had felt the presence of a third sometimes beside us, but I needed him to sense it now, hoping still that he would be on my side, that he would join me in my search.

He turned, and spoke.

'I forgot to ask you, Maeve. You did pack your pills, didn't you?'

'Yes, I did,' I said, loosing his hand, 'but in fact I threw them away just now, down into the harbour from the ramparts.'

V

Notwithstanding the nauseous heat and the boredom of remaining prostrate, I do not think that we should have travelled beyond the hotel and its immediate surroundings: the village, the stretch of coast road along which the mopeds bounced, the beach with its well-regulated water sports. The old streets of the town, the imposing fort and the colourful crowd were perhaps worth the visit we made there that first day, but anything else was definitely a mistake. Maeve is not so strong, after all. Even when we followed the tourist trail into the old quarter, she seemed ill at ease. Further on, at the spring, I thought for a moment she might faint, but it was I who became dizzy and disoriented.

Then, in the evening, she dropped her vial of pills at the fort above the harbour, and although I went back to find it, there was too little light left on the ramparts to make anything out. The one chemist still open for business at that hour refused to give me a replacement, polite but firm behind his shiny counter.

'But, look,' I said, 'here's the prescription, up-to-date. You'll find it's all quite correct.'

The young man spoke English perfectly, but he was having some trouble reading the handwriting on the paper I had carefully folded into my wallet before leaving home. He looked up from the prescription on the counter to where Maeve admired the perfume display.

'I cannot. I am sorry.'

Instead, all I could prise from him was a heap of equipment designed to foil the insects: lethal sprays, soporific smoke coils, pungent tubes of ointment. As I discovered that night, and all the nights that followed, these medicaments served rather to attract than repel their intended targets. The winking grey spirals puffed clouds of nasty smoke at my face; the vapour from the sprays made my eyes stream and my throat constrict. But still the ants

marched across the floor and up the wall, falling into the bed-
clothes whenever my eyelids drooped shut; and, as soon as the
light was turned off and the windows and doors stiflingly sealed,
the random whine of cruising mosquitoes would begin.

Often, after lying awake for hours above the rythmic beat from
the bar, I would finally doze, only to waken again in the darkest
part of the night with the drenched sheets clinging between my
knees and under my arms. I would sit up and swing my arms
above my head, hearing no sound, as yet feeling nothing, but sure
that I had just fallen victim to another blood-gorging raid. Gradually my arms and ankles became dotted with itchy spots which
merely spread into blotches when calamine or anti-histamine
were applied. Maeve for some reason was luckier, but even she
did not escape entirely.

In private, I could give vent to my urges and scratch, although
I quickly learned that the short-term relief would bring greater
suffering in the days to follow. The evenings were worse, spent
sitting in a bar or a taverna trying not to reach for the embarrassing
places and reminded continually of the night to come by the
flytraps which hung everywhere. Blue, fluorescent and terrifying
grids, they struck up a medley of sparks and sizzles under the
onslaught of bumbling moths, showing the smaller flying things,
the efficient attacking swarms, how to slip safely through the
heated filaments.

The courier had no advice to give. Her eyes were dull with
boredom, she had been worn down by the heat and the harass-
ments of several summers; now she was preoccupied with gathering as much commission as possible from the trips and the
car-hire special offers.

'My, you've really been bitten, haven't you?' was all she said
as we arrived at the mid-week information session in the lobby.
Then she turned back to the desk and resumed the taking of
deposits. The other members of our group gazed in silence at my
swollen arms and legs: I had rolled up the ends of my trousers to
exhibit my sufferings as far as decently possible. As we sat down
in the front row, I thought I heard a snicker or two.

'Perhaps I should have enquired about her sympathy level
before I booked the holiday,' I said to the man in the seat beside
me. Then I saw that it was Harry, and bit my lip.

'I'd keep out of the sun for a while, if I were you,' he said,
nodding solemnly at his audience. His own tan was by now that
of a year-round Californian surfer. 'Bound to irritate, y'know.'

'The sun doesn't agree with him anyway,' Maeve said, looking
up brightly from the folder of suggested day trips. Then I caught
her eye, and she coughed away her next words and turned back

to the itineraries, apparently absorbed by the careful photographs.

When I was winding up my complaint to the courier, in private this time, after the others had left, Maeve crept up beside me.

'I was just wondering, do you think we should take one or two of these trips, dear?'

'Sheer robbery.' I spoke to her out of the corner of my mouth, although by now I did not really care whether or not the courier might hear me. Maeve, however, was not deterred: my tone must have been softened by the lowering of my voice.

'How much is the car hire per day?' she asked.

'There's a special offer — three days for the price of two,' the courier said, and waited hopefully, but Maeve's polite silence and my amazed one made her reach in a tired way for the price-list.

'We'll think about it, thank you very much,' I said, snatching the paper from her fingers before Maeve could do so.

It was to be a brief victory. Three days later, as I lay in the dim bedroom, Maeve came in from the beach and threw her towel on the floor.

'How are your bites today, dear?'

'The same, the same. They're all right once I don't sit in the sun or get into the sea.'

Then she came and sat on the end of my bed. The peculiar tang of the Ionian Sea rose fresh and salty from her skin. Weakened by the unending heat and the mad swarms of insects, I could no longer resist her.

'It would only be for a day, dear. We could visit the mountains in the centre and maybe even the villages on the far coast.'

I merely grunted, engaged in trying to relieve an itch on my right instep.

'It's ridiculous the way it is. Honestly,' she gave a small laugh, 'I'll be picked up if I go to the beach on my own any more ....'

I stopped scratching and made a quick calculation of the minimum concession necessary to make me seem generous.

'All right, then. Half a day, for the mountains. I'm sure we can visit the other places by bus.'

I had, of course, no intention of spending any time at all on local jolting bus trips. Beautiful the far coast might have been, even with its hilltop monastery to climb to, but I was heartily sick and tired of the scenery everyone praised. I longed only to return to the cool mists of home, to resume the usual routine of my life.

This determination not to travel was to be reinforced by the four hours we spent in that inferno of a car, toiling up the scrubby, uninteresting mountains. There were no views of any significance to repay the intrepid driver; in any event, in the absence of lay-bys, there was no moment when I could lift my gaze from the centre of the narrow tracks designated on my map as 'second class roads'. But, by then, I had already agreed to take the bus and travel across to the opposite coastline. Maeve had won, taking advantage of my guilt as we drove away in the hired car from the hotel.

I had, I admit, snapped a little after the courier had departed and I was able to examine properly the wretched vehicle which had been palmed off on us. Nonetheless, I had often been brusque with Maeve in the past — not without extraordinary provocation, believe me — and a simple apology, with or without a quiet hug as circumstances demanded, was always sufficient to right the balance.

I suppose my agreement was prompted by the fact that Maeve seemed particularly interested in the other side of the island, and what she might really be thinking had come to dominate my days alone on the bed in the shuttered hotel room. She had spoken of an ancient legend, the beach beneath the monastery being the site of Ulysses' meeting with Nausicaa, or something of that sort. I must say that I still do not understand the increasing attraction those gods and heroes seemed to have for her; their trivial deeds, after all, had no basis in fact, only a setting of a lonely beach or a secluded spring in a clearing. Mere imagination, I say — or a useful mask for those who wish to hide their true concerns.

Give me, on the other hand, a decent walled town, a map showing early churches scattered among modern shopping centres, and I am a happy man. I am afraid that the island's main town proved to be neither very beautiful nor walled, and its places of worship generally unremarkable, no more than one or two centuries old. When, still hopeful, I sought assistance on more venerable monuments, the courier smiled blankly.

Eventually, I approached the proprietor who frowned seriously at my mime of praying hands. My knee had touched the floor of the lobby briefly, the chill lingering as I straightened, before I thought to wonder if he would know what I meant. The rite he followed might not include such gestures. But he nodded and swept his arm behind him, apparently to indicate the path around the outside of the hotel and back into the straggling olive orchards. It was then only fifteen minutes before the hired car arrived for our half-day trek into the mountains.

'Is it far?'

He frowned again and tapped his fingers on the reception desk.

Outside, there was quietness and I heard no traffic from the main road as I found the grassy strip leading towards the olive groves. The scrub at my feet rustled and I edged sideways, but it was only a scrawny hen shaking off sleep.

It was not very far to the church. The path broadened into a tidier paving after a couple of hundred yards and a belltower rose above the trees. I circled the building, passing a dusty porch, searching for a less neglected opening. There was, however, only the one entrance, a low bolted door under the faded tiles. A lizard scuttled away from it as I examined the keyhole. I placed my palms against its curling paint and shoved; it was only then, realising how foolish I might look to any observer, that I thought to shoot back the bolt and turn the handle. The door remained immovable and, after a moment, I stepped back out of the porch.

It was to be the first of the series of disasters over the last few days of the holiday. I am not a fanciful man, but it has occurred to me since that my failure to gain access to that church, an insignificant enough incident in itself, nonetheless heralded all that was to come.

As I turned back towards the hotel, a woman passed the other side of the church. She walked slowly, burdened with a full pail of water.

'When does it open?' I shouted to her across the clearing. She stopped, frightened at my stranger's voice, then looked up at the bell and shrugged indecipherably. I pointed and waved, trying again.

'When open? Open?'

She smiled while I glared at her helplessly, then she shifted the bucket in her hands and moved on, disappearing into the trees. I crouched and leaned my back against the wall, feeling the white-wash crumble and watching the ants gather hurriedly at my feet. After a while, I heard a car, the hired car presumably, turn into the hotel entrance, closer than I had imagined, only a minute's walk away.

Maeve was taking the keys from the courier.

'My wife is not the driver,' I said as I held out my hand. There was a small silence.

'Well, have a nice day,' said the courier as she walked over to the waiting taxi. 'And be careful of some of the roads — they're not very well surfaced.'

As we drove along the coast, searching for the turn to the hills, my disappointment at the closed church lessened somewhat and I realised that I had been unnecessarily rude.

'I'm sorry, Maeve.'

'For what?'

'It's probably better that I drive, you know. After all, I'm the one who brought the licence.'

She was silent, and I could hear the engine missing a beat. It was then that I rushed ahead, not thinking carefully enough, wanting only to smooth things over.

'What about a trip to that monastery some time? We could

spend the day there, you'd like that, Maeve.'

'If you wish.'

But, after another minute or two of hiccoughing plugs and points, she relented.

'That would be nice.'

All through the morning of baking, hilly tracks, I glanced sideways at her from time to time. She was more silent than usual, but there was something more to it, some expression of her face that seemed different when viewed from a certain angle. I suppose that was really why I agreed to drag my tired, bitten limbs on a two-hour bus trip each way. I wanted to find out her reason for going there, to put a halt to the separate lives we had been leading more and more during our stay on the island; almost since the first day, it seemed.

Even in the twilights, when I felt able to move about, Maeve had taken to wandering off on her own — along the beach and such places, she said. Last night, she had spoken of wanting to stroll up the hill at the back of the hotel, although she must have known that I would not wish to accompany her. After all, what was there to discover in that wilderness except farms or briars and a more intense heat even than on the coast?

Yes, I think that was it: I wanted to know what she found so fascinating about the empty woods and the far beaches; she must surely have known the island too well already from the last time she was here, in the days before her life and mine were fully intertwined. I had not yet, however, been able to prise from her even such simple facts as where she had stayed.

'It was all so strange to me, I was so young then,' was all she would say. 'I don't remember any of the sights — it was all sun, sea and sand. It could have been anywhere.'

I thought that perhaps it was the far coast. She was too happy on the day we went there, almost excited as the bus swung out onto the road which ran across the island from east to west, from the main town to the remotest villages.

The coach swept smoothly along the first stretch of low, scrubby hills, rocking me gently but insistently where I stood among the crowd of shopping-laden locals. I leaned down over her to peer through the gaps in the blind, unable to make out in the tame scenery whatever she stared at. Then the bus creaked over the final ascent of its route and plunged downward away from the smooth tarmac, beginning to jerk and groan as the landscape changed and rose to meet us in tree-clad rocky waves. When the sea appeared, just after I had managed to get the seat behind Maeve, I was prepared to give in gracefully.

'I have to admit it's very pretty,' I said into her ear.

'It's a world-famous beauty spot.'

But it was another tourist who answered me, while Maeve turned to look down at the cars and mopeds accelerating past in the narrow road. Then I felt the bus itself pull out almost into the far ditch, but carefully, lumberingly as befitted its bulk, to avoid crushing a fallen moped tangled with the limbs of its riders. As we passed, I glimpsed a girl clutching at a skewed ankle, her face whitening and twisted.

'Did you see that?'

Those of us who had observed the reason for the bus driver's curving of the wheel looked quickly at one another, relieved that we ourselves had not been down there, lying on the road. I was not sure if Maeve had seen or not: she had merely pushed up her sunglasses briefly and glanced towards the glaring scene now far behind. Almost immediately she turned to the front again, gathering her bag and her straw sunhat in one hand, her other tightening around the metal bar of the seat.

But when I helped her down from the steps at the beach, her body felt rigid, perhaps in delayed shock.

'I think the girl on the moped was only slightly injured — her ankle, that was all.'

Overhearing my remark, one of the women from the bus took her arm and led her over to the low wall behind the bus stop.

'It's all right,' I could hear her saying, 'it was just so hot on the bus. Thank you.'

When I joined her, she said, 'Sorry about that. I seem to have a thing about accidents.'

Then she bent her head and began to search her bag.

'Did you bring the camera?' she said.

'Yes. — It's no wonder, after that awful drive the other day. I think we ought to sit over there in the shade for a while and study the view.'

When at last we strolled to the beach, it was after midday and the soles of our feet were burning on the pebbly sand.

'Do you feel up to visiting the monastery?'

'You go — I'll swim,' she said.

I went slowly up the twisting roadway, trying not to inhale the choking trails of the cars and mopeds which passed continually. The track was too small for its present traffic, steep enough to have been an arduous ascent for the original pilgrims and their mules.

I paused half-way up at a narrow parapet and looked out over the sea. Three hundred feet below was the beach where she lay, but I could not identify her among the black dots, some crawling, some motionless. A sweaty man in shorts and teeshirt staggered to a halt beside my shoulder.

'Why do they always build them on the tops of hills, eh?'

He was making an effort to be friendly, hoping for companionship on the rest of the climb, but I pretended I could speak no English, smiled politely and walked on, stepping more quickly until the turns hid the beach from sight. Up this far, the trees hung thickly across the promontory, leaving room only for the road; below the unguarded precipice the rocks dropped down to the sparkling sea.

Hearing the rumble of a large vehicle, I stepped quickly away into the wood, tripping in my haste over the bare roots of old trees. A tour coach groaned past me, its passengers dim behind the smoked windows. They seemed unconcerned by the dangerous ascent, confident that the squealing brakes would anchor them to the rocky slopes long enough to reach the top. Looking back through the dusty air to where the road twisted out of sight behind the pines, and the sea hung waiting beneath, I thought that they might be more afraid on the return trip.

The headland was flat on top, filled by a small square before the closed monastery gates, and those few of us who had climbed on foot from the beach sat down with relief on the wooden benches or walked about in the shade on legs suddenly become rubber. I looked for a café or a water tap, but the monastery was the only sign of civilisation, the people descending from the bus or parking their mopeds near the greenery the only inhabitants of the silence. I waited until the tour group had passed through the entrance and then wandered over after them. A tall monk was about to bar the gate and waved his hand threateningly at me when I tried to slip past him. Two or three other late arrivals gathered behind me and together we listened to the bolt slotting into place behind the iron grille.

I spent a few moments in front of the bilingual notice, disentangling the familiar lettering from the indecipherable Greek script. The monastery, it appeared, shut promptly each day at one o'clock. It was now five minutes past the hour.

I was reluctant to turn back again, however; the rest of the day stretched emptily ahead until the bus trip back to the town and on to the hotel. I did not find the prospect of hours on the beach below very attractive, with Maeve engrossed in her thoughts and the chattering family groups around us giving me a headache.

Then, suddenly, I found an idea to ease the pull at the back of my thighs on the steep descent. I would telephone the office, I decided, and discover my good news in advance, rescuing the last days of the holiday from apathy, providing an excuse to make Maeve pay attention to me again. There would be plenty of time for queueing in the post office if we took the early bus from the beach to the town, plenty of connections on to the hotel.

When I sank onto the sand beside her, Maeve did not seem reluctant to leave the beach early, her previous anxiety to see the place evaporated under the boiling sun.

'Must be the hottest day yet,' I heard others in the bus-queue remark as the afternoon sweat trickled down our bodies beneath our clothes.

The temperature seemed higher than ever as we waited in the post office to make a second assault on the row of cubicles — the first attempt had got me no further than the office switchboard before the receiver went dead.

'Who was that girl?' I asked Maeve as she rejoined the top of the queue with a fresh handful of change.

'An Australian. Doing Europe. — By the way, she's invited me to trek on with her to Athens tomorrow.'

We laughed together. It struck me that it was the first time in days we had done so. I wondered if that moment might offer an opportunity to begin dismantling the barricades she had been stealthily building between us, but a telephone box had suddenly become vacant and she gave a warning pull at my jacket, then turned away.

'I hope we get through this time,' I said, stepping forward quickly, 'it's costing a fortune.'

John was my occasional confidant in the office when he was not being too pessimistic; like me, he had more than served his time on the lower floors of the organisation. He seemed unsurprised to hear my faint voice, almost as if he had known I would ring. My stomach tightened in anticipation.

'John — it's Tom. I didn't think I'd get you there. You're not about to head off or anything?'

I thought I heard him shifting papers with his free hand, ready for the rush out the door for the train.

'God, no. We're only just back from lunch here. How's the holiday?'

'Fine, just fine. Sun and sand, and all that. How are things in the office?'

'Well, you've heard about Anna, I suppose?'

'Yes? I mean, no. What about her?'

'Didn't you know? Thought that's why you rang. To get the low-down on Breslin. Hee, hee!' He interrupted himself with the knowing chuckle which always peppered his tales of the high flyers. As an unspoken rule, we never discussed the other kind, our fellow sufferers.

'Hello, still there?'

'Yes, go on.'

' — Sorry. I'd better fill you in, from the top. Anna got the promotion, of course. Straight upstairs, end of next month. Watch her in another five years ....'

'Who's this Breslin character?' I was suddenly aware of the hot stench of stale sweat deposited in the narrow cubicle by hundreds of previous users. I thought of the germs which might lurk in the mouthpiece an inch from my lips, and I tried not to breathe too deeply.

'Breslin? Breslin's your new section head, man. Oh, Christ, Tom, that's why you rang — .'

The sympathy sliding into his voice made me physically ill, and I thought that if I did not leave the phone box immediately I might actually throw up. I opened the door on the cacophony of voices, closing doors and rope soles on linoleum; then I lowered my voice enough to be audible but convincing.

'Listen, John, the connection's very bad and I've run out of change. I'll talk to you next week, okay?'

If you'll be seen talking to me, I thought as I replaced the receiver and turned to see Maeve's stricken face. As we pushed through the crowd around the doorway, she whispered something that could have been 'I'm sorry, Tom,' but I pretended not to notice.

'There's plenty of time before we head back to the hotel, and I need a drink,' I said, 'preferably a long, cool one.'

We sat for a while beside the main promenade of the town, beneath the high walls of the old fortress. It was lunchtime at home, late afternoon here, but the heat was more intense than the hottest noon that would ever be felt in the lower-floor offices. Even under the shade of the wide trees the sun made the raked sand warm the soles of our sandals and the metal of the old iron tables was tepid to our bare elbows. But, after two quick glasses of beer, the shock was fading with the smell of the cubicle in my nostrils, becoming just another part of next week's routine. I had, after all, gone through plenty of similar experiences during my years in the organisation and survived. Then I noticed Maeve folding up a sheet of thin paper and putting it into an airmail envelope.

'What's that?'

'Oh, nothing. I thought to ask at the post restante while you were queueing — force of habit, I suppose. It's from Danny ....'

Her voice trailed off, so that I was lulled into a pleasurable anticipation.

'Thoughtful of him, all the same. What does he say?'

Then she came out with it.

'They're getting married.'

'Who are?'

'Danny and Miranda — over there. In America. Next week, it says here.'

She unfolded the paper again and read the date at the top, while I stared at her, trying to work things out. Then she dropped the letter on the table between us and snatched at the brim of her hat instead.

'Next week?' I said.

'Next week, yes. Or, rather, this week by now —.'

'But how will we get there in time? Why didn't he give us more notice?'

I tried to think what arrangements could be made: flights, more leave, clothes if we went direct. Then I realised that Maeve was glaring across the table, as if willing me to release my mind from the list which was already forming.

'Don't you understand? He doesn't say where it is, or even what date. We're not going, because we aren't being invited.'

Her voice had risen slightly. I knew that the people at adjoining tables were looking over at us, two mad middle-aged tourists about to cause a scene. There was a throbbing silence until she spoke again, her voice pulled back to its usual levels, perhaps a shade too emphatic.

'I'm afraid there's no question of going,' she said.

I listened to her next words, her normal tone of voice, in disbelief. 'Do you think we should telephone them? Or, I suppose, a telegram might be more appropriate. A couple of lines, something nice ....'

'What are you talking about?'

The way Maeve had plucked calmness from a place I could not reach panicked me.

My rage hissed through my teeth, meeting the tiny breeze which was rising from the harbour and idling its way to our table. Like the slowly stirring air, my exhalations brought no relief, serving only to draw the flagging attention back to the persistent heat. I became aware that she was speaking again.

'I suppose it's all right. Isn't it? Miranda's a good girl, she'll look after him. I just wish that, maybe ... if they'd waited a while ....'

For a moment my fingers clenched the edge of the table until it rattled. I had the strange feeling that Maeve was not even trying to be calm, that after the first shock she had no need to hold back tears.

'Doesn't it bother you at all,' I said, in a low, clear voice which seemed to carry for miles, 'doesn't it matter to you that our son, our only son, won't even invite us to his wedding? Or that he announces it a week ahead — a day, maybe? Well? You're his mother after all. "Danny this, Danny that, Danny the other —." '

'You mean — Oh, you don't think they had to get married, do you? That would explain — .'

She seemed determined to defuse my anger, and I did not want her to.

'I don't think. No, he waited until he knew we were away, trapped in this godforsaken place. He knows what he's doing, all right. Knows what we'd say if given the chance.'

'But — Miranda's a lovely girl.'

I sighed and let myself slump in the metal chair. It struck me that Maeve had known all along how something like this would happen, how eventually we would be left with a collage of American grandchildren, brown-limbed and freckle-faced at the end of another, far-away summer. Small strangers would fill the closing pages of the photo albums.

As the chatter rose again from the neighbouring tables, I watched her for a sign, the least gesture that meant she would be there with me as the last prints were pasted in, but her eyes were opaque among the shifting shadows of the trees. When she spoke, I could not take in what she said above the strident whisper of the leaves. It sounded like 'Jason and Medea married here, they say.'

'What was that?'

She leaned forward, her elbow firmly on the table among the white rings of old beer-stains.

'I said, I wonder if they'll get married in a church?'

'That doesn't really matter, does it?' was all I could think of to say. 'That's not the point.'

Moisture trickled through the hot stubble between my nostrils and my upper lip, and the dregs of my lukewarm beer were no longer refreshing. Maeve was quiet now, the guidebook propped open on the table. As I spread my worn map over my knees, the waiter obediently advanced with his tray and removed the heap of coins on the saucer. I thought suddenly of the immediate future with relief. Tomorrow and all the days after that he would still be pacing up and down his patch of gravelled territory, but we would not be here.

Then Maeve said, 'You know how sorry I am about it all, don't you?'

As I stood up from the table, I reached for her free arm and held it tightly clasped to my side. Although she did not respond, I was still hoping that all it needed was a little effort until I had everything ironed out, until we were safely home and the past had been exorcised.

54

VI

When, at the end of the second week, the English group went home, the dining-room was almost empty. Although it was still only mid-season, I thought that after we in our turn had retrieved our passports from the desk and dragged our luggage out to the waiting coach, there might not be anyone left in the place.

The hotel was an afterthought on the edge of tourist civilisation. Perhaps it had been the first and only step in an over-ambitious spreading beyond the village shops and tavernas, up the hillside away from the sea. But now there was nothing else there except the solid three-story facade and, in the middle of the yellowed grass at the back, the undisturbed swimming pool. I had wanted to use it, but the waiting emptiness of the garden made me feel conspicuous. The visitors to this island, as elsewhere, seemed to be largely content with the sun and the sea; they were anxious to remain within sight of the beach or at least to feel beneath their sandals the crunch of sand as they strolled the short distance along the road towards the flashing taverna signs.

On our previous holidays together, we too had always kept to the well-worn path of local sights between the mini-market and the beach. This time, however, things were different. After the first day in the town, he had seemed consumed by something, perhaps it was the heat, or the insects, and he did not want to venture beyond the bedroom, except for our walks to the village for dinner. I, on the other hand, wished to explore the hillside, driven to move always inward. On our last evening, needing more than ever to free myself from his gaze, I left him resting in the room and closed the door softly behind me.

As I stood for a moment in the corridor, I could hear him shifting about inside and I felt panic as though I had left precious heirlooms unattended in a vast railway station where any one of thousands of transient thieves might see them. But I knew it was merely an unfounded attack of nerves, like one of those which used to make me reach for the pills. Since my first day back on the island, despite my growing fear, I had somehow felt the need of such crutches less and less.

I stood for a while in the windowless passage and waited for my rapid heartbeat to slow. After all, I no longer kept a diary, and there was nothing he could find among my possessions. I could do little about my actions: I was sure he must feel my drawing back these past few days, especially when I refused to humour him and visit the monastery on the tall cliff. However, he had pretended no surprise.

'It's really much too hot.'

'Well, if you don't want to.... I'll be off, then. After all, it's what we came here for, there's not much else, is there?'

Afraid to breathe, I did not argue with him or speak up in favour of the famed tiny bays set like sapphires into the luminous green hills. I did not speak at all, I merely laid my towel flat on the sand at one end of that particular cove and tried to keep my eyes from flickering over and back across the jagged rocks at the foot of the cliffs. The paraphernalia of suntan lotions abetted my mime of uninterest and at last he left, stepping quickly through the prone bodies and the abandoned sandcastles.

Turning away on one elbow, I removed his guidebook from the net bag, surprised that he had forgotten it. Although he could not possibly see my face, yet I feared his discovery more than ever as he toiled up the winding roadway around the headland, thinking, unimpeded by my presence. There would certainly be a viewing spot half-way up, and, if he had forgotten to bring his binoculars to inspect the scenery, plenty of other tourists along the way to lend a pair.

But my need drove me, and I folded the book into the towel and walked back along the beach to the village. It was a cluster of houses set behind stone walls, two tavernas, a shop. I did not dare to enter the yards of the shuttered houses where nothing, not even a scrawny chicken, moved. Instead, I bought an ice-cream in the shop and sat on the wall near the larger taverna while I unwrapped the paper. It was now lunchtime, and the tables were occupied with dozens of sightseers trying to fill up the hours before the next bus to town.

The staff had quickened their usual stroll to a slow trot, and the high cheekbones above the moustaches were silvered with sweat. A woman serving a table near the wall was more active than the men, even though she was small and plump, and burdened by a dark dress of heavy material. She reminded me of Milly and, as she moved past the nearest table, she smiled at me in the same way.

Within less than a minute, what was left of my melting ice-cream had slipped from its stick to the ground, drawing a trail of ants like a magnet. I had no further excuse to sit there, so I stood and smoothed my skirt; then I returned down the dazzling road to the beach.

As I dragged my towel from the bundle and shook out the sand, the guidebook fell from its folds. I picked it up and laid my body down among the sunbathers. Dust or tears pricked my eyelids as I opened the first page. I blinked, to erase from my mind the faces of the men in the taverna, like brothers with the same unruly black or greying hair, those faces which had not recog-nised me, nor I them. Only the woman who could have been their older sister had smiled, and her gesture, in its careless sponta-neity, had shown me that my dream was an illusion, that none of these people were anything more than strangers, nor ever could be.

The guidebook was more distracting than I had hoped. It spoke of the ancient legends of the island, Ulysses tossed by the waves to the feet of Nausicaa, the passing of the Argus, the wedding of Jason and Medea in the Temple of Apollo which even then was old .... The sketch of the mythic landscape was crudely drawn, but its very terseness inspired me to imagine the whole island, coasts, town, lagoon, empty of tourists, awaiting still the farmers and fishermen, a lush playground for the gods.

What occurred later on in the afternoon when we went again to the town, the series of bad tidings from home, or what had once been home, was merely the last dismantling of the framework, leaving us on the brink of discovery. In my dreams afterwards, I did not know whether I wanted to step forward or turn back. Perhaps I had already chosen without realising it, when he brought me to the spring where the temple once stood, and we drank there. Or, perhaps, my path had been laid out for me long before, and I had never really shaken off its dust from my sandals since the first time when I had hesitated and turned back at the edge of the clearing.

This time, I did not want to leave the cool, hidden grove where the water flowed from the earth, but he spun so unsteadily in search of the exit that I took pity on him, even though I knew he was already suspicious enough to destroy me. Now, after the steady pressure of his gaze from the headland, and the long, close bus ride back across the spine of the island, I needed to get away from him, to place my feet along the secret paths.

Each twilight, we had seen the proprietor of our hotel sitting in the gravelled courtyard, looking out onto the steep rutted track and listening with a sad air to the thrum of disco music which rose from the village below to drown the call of his own amplified chords. Tonight, when I stepped from the cool emptiness of the lobby into the evening's warm twilight, I smiled and nodded at him to offer encouragement.

'Good evening, madame,' he said in a BBC accent, but I had already discovered that he spoke almost no other English.

As I turned through the spotted iron gates, thinly painted white over old rust, the rising hill and the thickly planted cypresses soon hid his white building and muffled the sounds from the village. In the greyness, the tarmac scuffed pale by winter rivulets merged into the dusty edgings. It seemed a path rather than a roadway, a clear way up the hillside barely tolerated by the spreading vegetation and the overhanging trees. After a few yards, even the whisper of constant traffic on the coast road below and behind vanished. No cars turned off to track me, since the rutted hairpin bends were sign-posted merely for an unimportant village several kilometres further inland.

Then, there rose from the foot of the hill a voice I had not heard for days.

'Maeve? May I join you?'

She panted up the road behind me, one hand pressed to her waist. I stopped to let her catch up; I even walked back a few yards to bridge the distance between us, so glad was I, despite my yearnings, to have her company, to protect me from the lure of the drop beyond the precipice.

'Hello, Milly,' I said as she reached me, 'Letty told us you'd been ill.'

'Yes — the sun, I'm afraid. Tom, too, I think?'

Her nose was peeling, but otherwise she seemed untouched, her arms and legs as fair-skinned as when we had arrived. I wondered if she really had been ill, or just unable to forget what she had left at home.

'How's Ginnie? Better, I hope.'

'Well ....' In her struggle between politeness and the urgency of truth, I could feel myself weighed and tested.

'Ginnie's not very well, you see. I don't think she's going to get better.'

She cried then for a while and I stood beside her with my arm half-around her shoulder, feeling a pulse beating beneath her skin.

With the onset of night, the cicadas were silent and the crickets had not yet begun their friendly scraping. Or perhaps there were no crickets up there, since it seemed that there was usually no one to listen to them. As we descended around the bends of the road, I could hear only Milly's ragged sighs. Then, at the last turning, I could just catch the whispers fading on the hillside behind, and I saw the breeze gathering the last of the early summer fireflies in among the leaves. Our steps slowed and we stood overlooking the white roof of the hotel. Milly was quiet now, and, for a moment, all movement in the trees around us ceased. I held my breath: it was almost too still.

Then the record turntables turned together and the complex silence of the night drowned beneath the disco beat, and we moved forward to the iron gates. By now it was thickly dark, and the proprietor's chair was gone from the gravel.

'Good evening, Madame. — And to you also, Madame.'

He was now behind the reception desk. Then, in a less formal tone, he added, 'Boom, boom,' as he pointed upward and outward.

'A storm. He means we're going to have a storm tonight.'

The tall Englishman whose name was Harry had approached the desk and grinned ingratiatingly. He, it seemed, had not departed with the rest of his tour. His wife stood watchfully beside him. Indignant, she glanced at the proprietor who was looking at their lips move while smiling and bobbing his head.

'Oh no, I hope there isn't going to be thunder and lightning. I hate thunder and lightning.'

'Yes, yes. Boom, boom.'

As we climbed the stairs, I strained to hear any rumbles outside, but my ears were deadened by the inevitable beat of the music from the bar.

'Goodbye, Milly,' I said when we stood outside her door. 'And say goodbye for me to Letty.'

I felt a strange sense of doom at the thought that she was leaving the island later that night, almost as though it were I and not her unknown sister who was dying.

'I'll write to you,' she said as she lifted her key, but I was not sure if she would.

In the room, the light was on and the balcony curtain blew in and out through the open door, curling in the newly revived breeze. He was fastening the buttons of his shirt, pink and rested after his nap and his cool bath, readying himself for the walk down to the row of competing tavernas.

'Is it still warm? Will I need my jacket tonight, do you think?'

I lay on the bed, unlatched the straps of my sandals, and told him about the storm. As I spoke, I could feel it coming, the clouds moving together above the thickening air; even in the stone-tiled room, it was becoming more and more humid. I was languid with waiting as I leaned my head on the pillow and closed my eyes.

'Better shut the balcony door before we go. Are you ready?'

With an effort, I raised myself from the bed and put on my straw hat; it was the only defence against the forthcoming weather I intended to muster, merely a gesture for his sake. When the rain tore itself free of the clouds, I wanted to feel it lashing on my hair and running down my temples, like the spray from a wave breaking on a rocky shore.

But it was long after we returned to the hotel, when he had slumped against the wall in silence, and I sat on the side of the bed and stared at my hands swinging between my knees, that I heard the first drops splatter onto the balcony floor. The storm had broken at last, the stark revelatory flashes already waning and the roar overhead now a faint grumble over the straits. As the rain steadied itself against the dying wind, its battering of the trees and the window glass seemed the echo of a more northerly season. But I knew that when the shower stopped, and the curtain was raised and the glass door rolled back, the warm miasma of the island would be sucked into the room to wipe away the chill of autumn, but not the old and threadbare yet invincible grey mist which hung between us.

While I waited, I tried to think what I was to do. As I sat facing his corner, I wondered if I should have acted on the day of our expedition to the mountains, seized the steering wheel of the hired car and wrenched it to the left, to where the road crumbled away at the edge into chasms. I knew that he would not have been able to react in time: since the beginning of the drive, his eyes had remained locked onto the climbing twists of the rutted track, to the few solid metres ahead along the central line where the axle-wrenching potholes were less thick, before the steepness of the incline snatched the road from sight around yet another hairpin bend. I also knew that the handbrake did not work and that there was only a tentative balance between the forces of gravity exerted by the slope we were climbing and the pull of the fully extended footbrake.

'Get out,' he had almost screamed at me, when the car stalled the first time on a forty-five degree bend and the handbrake's creaking addition to the footbrake made no difference to the slow, but gradually accelerating, trickle backward of the wheels. I was so surprised at his lack of composure that I obeyed, although I realised as I looked up and down the dusty track that he had become more frantic with each passing day on the island, circling around my secret but unable yet to guess the last turnings of the maze.

Suddenly, I opened the door and got back into the car.

'What the hell do you think you're doing?'

'Reverse slowly backwards,' I said, 'until we come to a flat part.'

He ignored me, pulling sharply again and again on the handle beside my knee, the footbrake pedal still firmly to the floor, no doubt hoping to stretch them to some point beyond even the manufacturer's knowledge, to where they would eventually conquer the mountain. Then, when he tried to start the car, he had to release the brake pedal. As the plugs and points coughed briefly and became silent, the car slipped several feet backwards towards the edge and the rocky scrub below. After five more minutes, the engine took and held and we crawled forward into the centre of the road again.

So it went on for more than an hour, until we reached the peak of the pass and swung down the gentler bends on the other side. I would have had plenty of opportunities: we passed no other cars and only one group of workmen who tinkered lazily with the foundations of a villa near a ruined farmhouse. They had not even looked round as we passed on one of the more extended bursts of forward momentum, busy as they were with a slow bending to pluck sound bricks from the heaps of rubble under the olive trees.

While I stared through my passenger window at the cliff of yellow rock and listened to the grinding of the brake cables, I thought how easy it would be to jerk the wheel free during the next tortuous stage of the ascent, how simple a way to do it. The terrain, the fact that it was a hired car, the heat of the day: all these would reassure the police, even save Danny too much trauma. Though why I thought at that moment of lessening Danny's guilt I no longer know.

In the end of course, I did nothing. Perhaps I had never intended to, after all; on that final evening of the fortnight, I could easily have been prey to such imaginings, prompted by a random memory, an accident on the road as our bus passed, or children playing on the cruel rocks at the end of a golden strand: events involving some other's fear, someone else's life.

And, eventually, on the last night, at the moment when I thought I had flicked around the corners of the maze just in time, he came upon me. If any of those events I had seen snap the thread of others' lives had happened to me, he might never have known, but I was not convinced of final escape by that way; I was more sure of his doggedness, his ability to go on tracking me through the other labyrinth, the one on the far side of the darkness, its mirror image.

We had gone to a new place for our last meal of the holiday. It was he who had spotted the sign one day, and admired the tables almost hidden from the road by a thicket of cypress and a single chestnut tree. Now he argued its merits again as we walked beneath the grey sky to the village, although I was not attempting to demur. In my confused state of mind, I thought that a strange place might bind my tongue to caution where familiarity would lull it into unwariness.

He had led the way to the centre table under the thickest branches of the chestnut tree, picking up the wine list as he pulled his chair closer to the cloth. It was as if there was no time to lose before the final stages of the hunt.

'Spiro?' I asked, and he looked up, surprised no doubt that I already knew the waiter's name, perhaps scenting blood. My knees refused to bend, my fingers slackened on the back of the chair, all my armour pierced by the sudden dagger of recognition. The waiter raised his moustaches clear of brilliant teeth and reached to assist me. I noticed that he wore a faded blue shirt with metal buttons, a row of tiny shields in the last gleams of daylight. Looking into my own warped reflection along his torso, I suddenly realised that he was a complete stranger.

'Yes, Madame. I am Spiro. My son, too, is Spiro.' I followed his glance to a far table, where a silent youth in the usual loose white shirt and skintight black trousers dabbed at the crumbs with a cloth, then covered them with cutlery.

'Spiro is name of many men on the island, after our patron saint.'

The waiter drifted away towards the smoky doorway of the kitchen, ignoring frantic waves from other customers.

Across the table, he looked at me, waiting.

'I thought I knew him, from the last time.' I was conscious that I was speaking too fast, and I slowed my voice. 'But of course it wasn't really .... Did you know that every eldest son is called Spiro here?'

He looked down at the wine list again. When Spiro returned with the bread and the oil, I sat back and concentrated on his large hands adjusting plates and cutlery. I heard him say, 'Madame was here before.'

'Yes,' I said, 'but it was a long time ago. How did you know?'

'Ah,' said Spiro, spreading his fingers wide, 'you must, I think, have drinked at the spring of Kardaki.'

'The famous spring,' he said then, watching me still from the other side of the condiments and the fresh bread, 'three stars and three cheers for the famous spring.'

Spiro turned to him.

'It is such a beautiful land, my island, is it not? Beautiful enough for a honeymoon, I think.'

'We didn't — This is my first visit,' he said.

Spiro smiled down politely but firmly.

'But not the last. It is the saying here, he who drinks at Kardaki must return. Perhaps you may never leave us.'

As we poured the dressing onto our heaped plates, I felt the strong wine flush my face. The string of lights bobbed along the branches of the tree, keeping the cloudy night at bay, even warming his voice a little.

'Cold, dear? Put on my jacket if you like.'

'No — no, thanks. I'm too warm, if anything. This isn't the usual watery wine, is it? Dionysias would be proud of us.'

He smiled, filling our glasses again. Then he sat back and stopped twisting his fork through his plateful, and looked a little too carefully at me.

'I don't think somehow that "Spiro and Son" will ever be written over this taverna. By the look of it, Spiro junior won't be around very much longer. Athens, I suppose, or even America. What do you think?'

'I don't know,' I said, 'I hope not.'

'Twenty-five years ago, Spiro was young and tourism here was at its peak. Now, though .... Time can make such a difference in places, people, too. Would you agree with that, Maeve?'

I paused, uncertain how to reply, what to concede, bitterly regretting the longing which had made me falter, the fever which had led me to mistake Spiro for the cheerful waiter who had flirted impartially with all of us long ago. From his wild eyes inches from mine, rather than from the words of his question, I thought I knew what he was getting at; I could not speak, but I was afraid to look away in case I accidentally intercepted Spiro's gaze instead.

Although I was saved from any answer by the flying ants which came like a message from the hills to our very table and drove us away, I should have known that he would not leave it at that, I should not have been taken in by his pretended drunkenness. Murderers are always in control of themselves, and of others.

When we walked up the track from the village, he made as if to stumble on the boulders which gleamed against the dusk, but it was merely an excuse to clutch heavily at my arm and drag me closer to his side. Crushed against him, my body was awkward, my balance disrupted; and, in the end, it was I who really tripped on the sudden sharp protrusions of the road. As he pulled me to him again, it struck me that to the passing strollers we must seem a tipsy Darby and Joan, embracing on a fond second honeymoon.

Indeed, as I sat on the edge of the bed that night, and he began the questioning, it seemed for a moment or two that I could cry halt to our blind pursuit of disaster and rip off our tragic masks. I gazed clearly into my soul and saw not such a very big secret after all, surely not one which would cost me everything. But who can ever estimate the price to be paid for hope, or the ransom which the gods might demand if they still spoke to us?

VII

The cat sits and watches me from the front garden, through the
bay window. I do not know where it lives otherwise, only that
it leaps up surefooted onto the slanting window-sill at the same
time each afternoon and crouches there until the twilight shades
into complete darkness and I can no longer see its shape. It has a
faded orange fur spotted with dirt or paler markings, and its body
is rounder near the haunches, thin at the neck. It would be an
unremarkable feline, except that its eyes are huge amber prisms,
as if inherited from an Egyptian ancestor. In them I see preserved
my halting gestures of propitiation, for ever fragmenting, and
reforming; dissolved, then re-enacted.

The doctor suggested that I write it all down. Why, and what?
When I asked, she just smiled and gave me a blank pad to take
home.

'We recommend it — it might even help,' she said as she
walked in front of me to her office door and the telephone on her
desk began to bleep again. It had been disconnected when I sat
down into the curved chair and began to speak. As I closed the
door behind me and heard her answer it, it struck me that she
must have replugged it into the console when the half hour was
up, without my observing her gesture. I don't notice things so well
any more. That must be why Maeve managed to do what she did.

But — stop. I am doing it again, in just the same way as I tried
to tell the doctor. Leaping ahead. Blocked from taking it one step
at a time. You see, if I could just give them the photo albums it
would all be much simpler. Although now they lie under the bed,
mixed up with a heap of newspapers, magazines and old lists,
each one is numbered and they could be assembled easily into the
correct order by a stranger, the story straightforwardly told by the
series of images. But they do not want to know about the albums,
and I can only show them the scribbled notepad, the paper torn
with the efforts I made to get past the first few words. When I

handed it to her, that nice doctor, she kept it and gave me another. 'A block,' she said, 'try again.'

Blocked. What a solid word that is for the scratches I make on the new pages every day, unable to reconnect myself to the old order of things, the three pot plants I watered every five days in summer, less often in winter: they flourished in the ambient light and heat, guarded from the draught by the wads of paper I taped into the gap between the skirting board and the wall, between the window-frame and the glass. When the day eventually arrived that I got my promotion, I intended to tear away the insulation and let the plants fend for themselves: they had grown so large that the spider's webs among their foliage kept the light from my desk and its in and out trays, and they were too unwieldy to be moved elsewhere. In any case, my successor might not have wanted the trouble of watering them.

To think that I used to hope for freedom from that narrow room! Even when the whispers of the downtrodden clung to me in the corridor although I strode on to shake them off, I thought that at least I could retire from the struggle one day, take up my pen and walk away. This vision floated before me on summer mornings when sunlight burnished the filing cabinet and reddened the wood of Anna's desk; the lure of home in the unknown hours of the day, the invasion of the secret rituals of Maeve's life, the freedom to watch the early television programmes whose titles I studied in the newspaper.

When a colleague retired, I always attended the presentation, wondering at the lack of eagerness with which the proffered television set was seized upon, the long-drawn out speech which failed to bridge the gap between the applauding crowd and the single figure beside the gift-wrapped box. But I don't wonder any more.

They have been very kind to me in the office. Anna is already gone, and the new section head is managing my work — 'keeping things ticking over,' they say; but a man from personnel has sent me the organisation's terms for early retirement. They expect me back soon, my colleagues insist, on the card they sent from the section. But they sent with it a video-recorder, as if to spare me the rigours of a presentation ceremony.

I do little with all my extra hours of freedom. Several I spend in bed, clinging each morning onto the edge of the mattress and the fringes of sleep, my shoulder turned against the spaces of the day that await me. And yet I cannot find time now to watch those daytime television programmes. The minimal household tasks which are all I can accomplish are limitless, there is no out tray on my hall table into which I can fling the washing machine or the hoover when they have been used; instead, they wait there mutely, stripped of their former benevolence under Maeve's hand, resentful of my ignorant touch, outstaring me for hours on end.

So, I make use of the video they have given me, rerunning the tapes carefully to edit out the commercial breaks. I erase the squeaking toy voices and the jingles so that I can watch the films or the documentaries straight through without distraction, when I have time. But I never have time, and so a heap of recorded programmes fills the shelf below the television. I am running out of blank tapes.

I am sure that Maeve would have used the video more fruitfully: she would have hired old films to watch with her friends in the afternoons, leaving the washing-up and the dinner until just before she heard my key in the lock. Or perhaps she never had any friends in that way, I don't really know. No groups or individuals have come forward to identify themselves.

In fact, no one at all comes here to speak to me. Sometimes they telephone from the office; and once I made a call myself, long distance, through the operator, but Danny and Miranda were out. So I forced myself to write instead, to explain why we never congratulated them or answered their honeymoon card from Acapulco which lay in the hall when I returned.

Now I wait for a reply to my announcement, although the time I have calculated for two letters to pass forward and back has already elapsed. Each morning I hear the flap creak as I wake, and when I can make myself rise and descend the stairs, there is an envelope where it should be on the carpet. The name, however, is not mine, it is always for Maeve. At first I tore them open, hoping to find in the terse acknowledgements, the free recipe leaflets and the stencilled entry forms a clue to her defection, an entrée into her accumulated reasons for her actions. But these revelations of her other life only add to the long blankness beyond my former industry in the hive of the organisation, they confuse and do not convince.

One afternoon, the postman rang the bell and handed me a package which contained a plastic digital timepiece, but no other information. I put the watch into a spare drawer in the kitchen, hiding it beneath her old diary; I could not bear to see its soundless tick against my wrist. The diary itself had no recent entries, and served only to add to my bewilderment. I opened it and read a description of the changes in the evening sky between ten and ten thirty on the twenty-ninth of June several years previously. The entry continued over three pages, but there was no reference to any of the events I had noted for the same evening in my own pocket diary: washing the car, watching the news, trimming the lawn edgings.

A digital watch, a cat, accumulating dust. It seems that I can clearly remember only the actions which did not matter, the feelings which probably did not have any bearing at all on what actually happened. My life has been blown apart as easily as if it had taken hours rather than decades to construct, and the pieces still have not fallen back into place. As I pass through the rooms on my daily round, I hope that somewhere underneath the growing pile of paper on the hall table there is a single page which will explain it all to me.

What she told me in the hotel room on our last night together had been too sudden after the endless fortnight of escalating bewilderment: I failed to grasp the essentials. Instead, I saw only another sleight of hand, another tautly worded recipe which meant nothing to the novice but would have been everything to the initiate. Perhaps it was the insects which were to blame. I could not keep my eyes away from their sure progress of destruction nor wrench my mind from following their frantic lives of mutual genocide. They had already begun to obscure things in the taverna that night, flying thickly through the warm air around our table and swarming down over the tablecloth, darkening the twilight between us.

She had sat opposite me, pink and brown in her new sunfrock, and I was driven at last to think of her photo album, the concluding entries of smiling girls posing in turn for each other's camera. Then I had to ask, even though I knew she would not obey me easily. There had been, after all, plenty of opportunities, twenty-five years of them, but instead she had chosen concealment and distance.

'Tell me about it, Maeve, what it was like here all those years ago.'

She smiled, and frowned, and half-opened her mouth. It was then that the first insect floated before her face, drawn by the moisture of her lips.

We had not noticed their coming, but now they were all around, swarming from the tree, as usual escaping the electric fly trap in the branches. I brushed the first ones away from the table where they lay flapping their wings and moving their legs, as if not sure whether they should walk or fly. No one else seemed to pay any attention, but our plates soon became filled with the black creatures.

'Ugh,' said Maeve, noticing the number of them at last when a dozen more landed in the bread basket and several stuck themselves to the outside of the oil bottle. Any further talk was impossible, choked by tiny bodies and the throb of the bazouki music from the loudspeaker above our heads. We salvaged what we could from our plates and did not wait to finish the bottle of wine.

'They come, every year, down from the mountains,' the waiter called Spiro said as he flapped once or twice at the bread with a cloth, 'it's no harm.'

He seemed amused at our hasty departure, calling out to his son something which gave rise to mutual hilarity, and I wanted to strike him. A combination of tiredness and too much wine too fast, no doubt; but he deserved a lesson. As he followed us through the curious diners, it seemed that we alone had been singled out to sit in the path of the swarm.

'It's only the flying ants,' said a man at the edge of the court-yard, under the open sky. 'They pass this way, through the trees,' he was remarking to his companions as Maeve hurried me away through the dry electric air in which lightning danced.

As we struggled over the stones of the track from the village, my scalp still tingled with imagined crawling feet and feebly beating wings.

'That was horrible,' I said, turning to look at her and slowing my steps, but she would not speak.

Something that had always seemed permanent was slipping away, flopping and dying like the disoriented ants. In front of the barred gate of the monastery, I had already sensed what I was to discover that last night as the storm made suitable sound effects out on the balcony. What I had not foreseen as I tried to reason it out in the shade of the monks' lemon tree, on the seat where pilgrims now never sat, was how unsatisfying the final outcome would be, how eventual knowledge would lead me on to the brink of an even darker abyss. That the final moment of truth had already occurred, at Kardaki, I can see only now: standing over the fountain itself I was blinded by the light which trickled out of the cracked stones. As late as the last day, I had thought that despite Danny's defection, despite my ignominious return to the same desk, I could still have Maeve. Entering the café, before the meeting with Spiro brought it all to a head, my dazzled eyes looked on Maeve's fading presence and saw a bright loyalty.

Later that night, the storm broke and the heat abated at last. In the morning, I was chilly as I turned under the clinging sheet and saw the emptiness of her bed, its coverlet turned back. Her bags were gone, her make-up, even her toothbrush from the bathroom. Only her pink sunhat remained, hanging from the back of the door; for a moment, it gave me hope, but then I remembered she had hardly worn it during the past few days, acclimatised, she said, even to the midday glowing disk in the centre of the sky.

I missed my flight, of course. The courier, the police, everyone was kind, but the questions and answers took so long to pass forward and back in two languages. I stood in the middle of the hall after the other tourists had left, avoiding their backward glances and hearing their murmurings above the thump of suitcases into the hollow belly of the airport bus.

She had asked him to get a taxi, the proprietor said sadly, and the courier translated briskly; the taxi was for the town. They checked the ticket booths at the harbour, in case she had left the island that way; and then the check-in desk for flights to the mainland, or even to Italy. All that day, I sat in the hotel lobby, trying to think, so that I could tell the bustling, sweaty policeman something further. After they had all gone again, I went up to the room and sat out on the balcony, watching the serrated cypresses darken on the hillside, listening for the sound of her steps.

When another day had passed, they brought me to the airport, to a spare seat on a suitable plane. As I stepped through that ornate Venetian doorway for the last time, I saw Harry bow his head and turn away.

'You're a permanent resident, too, it seems,' I said as I passed him by.

I did not first think, even when I saw that her lotions were missing and her towel carefully removed, that she had the spirit to do it. It was when I sensed Harry's concern and saw the courier's efforts waning, the authorities drawing back, that I realised she was gone. Until then I had been passive, waiting amid the bustle with languid detachment, but now the determination grew in me to find her.

The man that the travel company had sent from Italy walked with me from the airport building over to the silver plane, as if to make sure that one of us at least went home. He told me that she could not possibly be on the island still, that they would have found her in two days. But with each step up the metal stairway from the tarmac I became more certain that they were wrong. As the plane banked, I looked down on the bright lagoon and the green hills beyond, and I knew that she was down there somewhere.

I remember the three hour flight back so clearly: the crying children, the red-haired hostess who brought me more beer. Or perhaps that was on the trip out, when she sat beside me looking out the window. I am not quite sure just at the moment.

Since my return to this house, they have sent a woman, one in a white dress they say is a nurse, to be with me always, even when

I pretend to sleep. She does not reply to my questions and she will not carry out the tasks of the house, although I have written the instructions on the notepad. Whole days I spend in this way, ignoring the stench of unwashed plates from the kitchen, transcribing schedules for the ordering of my life onto sheet after sheet of paper, even though I have already discovered that she will not pay any attention. Only the doctor surveys my plans, but the doctor does not seem to be interested in my priorities and simply smiles when I complain about the quality of nursing staff.

In the evenings, while the dead fireplace shivers ash onto the carpet, I turn my face to the gap between the sofa cushions and try to think it all out. But the woman in white watches me always, forcing my memory onward past important details as easily as pressing the fast-forward button on the video. Like a cat with a mouse she sits, poised on her haunches, watching me. I know her by now, I have learnt her ways by stealth, peering out through the cracks of light between my fingers in the lengthening evenings. Even though she cannot realise I am looking, she will maintain her mask, glancing away now and again, feigning lack of interest, waiting for me to relax my guard.

Strangely, she does not interfere if I leave the house, but I dare not do do very often, fearing that I will miss a vital communication. Although I know that Maeve will not return to me here, still I find it hard to believe absolutely; it is difficult not to hope that sooner or later some clue will lodge itself in my mind as easily as the leaves float down from the trees in the garden. Sometimes I have abandoned thought, closed the hall door softly behind me and followed mere instinct; I have gone along the shore to watch the sea, always accompanied by my guardian in her white dress.

As the plane rose from the island, I had a last glimpse of a tiny village with networked lanes, diminishing into a child's jigsaw and then vanishing as the pilot climbed into the sun. I get that same perspective now from the top of the sand-dunes between the coast road and the beach, when I look inland and see the lines of pretty boxes and the toy towers which decorate my horizon. There is the same sense of puzzlement as I felt when the plane spread the island below my window: I see but cannot recognise the landmarks which for such a long time have circumscribed my life.

As I go further down the beach to walk along the water and look outwards, the island seems more real than this mirage where I dwell; at times it might lie only a stone's throw away across the endless sea. I cannot yet glimpse the gods she worships, nor can I be certain of discovering alone the way through the twisting paths of the island. In that ancient place, a shadow glancing along

71

the rutted ground ahead may be all there will be as guidance, uncertainty my only companion. Despite my yearning, I am pinioned by my reason to habit and security; and, then, as I stand at the waves' edge I can feel the wind rushing southwards, scattering the flimsy pages of my life before it.

And of all my past only one memory seems worth fighting for, worth resisting the blandishments and the pills, even the final erasure of my notes by the woman in white. I can still taste that single moment of heat and coolness, of dust and moisture, when Maeve and I drank together below the temple. Unknown, unrecognised, the shades beckon me back to the narrow circle. I know, finally, that I must return there if I am to find her and make things whole again. I, too, have drunk at the spring of Kardaki.

VIII

It is a lost domain, the centre of this island, its stewards long migrated to the coastal strip or set sail on the sea which gleams around corners everywhere, leaving the lemons to wizen on the spreading trees and the olives to drop unheeded into the long grass. The scattered dwellings of the fled lie in ruins: shuttered with old boards half eaten by the rain and sun, demolished in purple gashes by the climbing bougainvillea and shattered by the outflung limbs of old trees.

Now I alone have returned to stroll in this neglected park, pushing aside the waxy leaves of oleander and castor oil plant from my path, peering from the road into dim, spreadeagled olive groves, through padlocked iron gates, down grassy lanes to a broken door-step. Yet, not I alone: everywhere, there are thin cats, bleached by the sun. Dusty whites or pale marmalades, they run along the road and leap the ditch into an overgrown garden, glancing back at me resentfully. At this season it is a park without many flowers to please these feline wanderers. The blossoms prefer the freshness of spring and the rains which bring a second burgeoning in autumn; this evening, there is merely the infinite shadings of green, the profusion of leaves and branches.

Constantly, the reminders of cultivation surprise me: the once-straight stone barriers through which the myrtle bushes root themselves, the crooked metal sign naming a village of broken-down walls. Here and there are signs of more recent visitation: a gleaming hump of new tarmac to mend a single pothole among the rest, a shimmering nylon net on the grass beneath an olive grove near the top of the hill. But among the arbutus trees with their too-abundant rosettes, the giant cypresses pointing silently up at the mink clouds, and the riot of brambles and ferns, such signs are powerless to dispel the laxness.

As I turn to walk away from this ungoverned wilderness, a cat crouches at shoulder level on a stone pillar, tenses, then leaps, about to sink its claws into my back and my arms ....

I always wake from this dream with my hands shaking the coverlet and the channel of my breast chill with rivulets of oily sweat. I have this experience almost nightly now, and only the symptoms of wakening vary: a numb arm twisted beneath my side, a cramped foot, aches in my ribs.

Once, when my innocence was as yet folded softly around my shoulders, there had been no nightmares, only the garden spreading itself at my feet.

Today, after the dream, I rose, and dressed, and pulled aside the curtain to see the day. The deep blue sky of early morning was lightly wrinkled, as if newly unfolded to dry off the dew. It was a moment of Indian summer in the middle of autumn; as I stood behind the glass and felt my body grow cooler, I could see the trails of cirrus rising from the western horizon, few as yet at this hour.

I left the bedroom and went to the kitchen, my head glowing in the first slicing sunbeams as I gathered and prepared food. The light caught the fittings of my machines and flashed arrows into my eyes. It is all just the same as before, you might say; but it is not quite the same.

I spent a lot of the first days in reading, learning more of the legends which began as my excuse for the trek from east to west of that island, but which ended by becoming the instruments of my enlightenment. Yet now, replete with pages of facts, I am less sure of anything. For it was not the truth behind events, mythic or otherwise, that I sought; I was content merely to savour the names. Jason, Medea, Ulysses, Nausicaa: these labels I could paste onto whatever phial of hope I chose to carry with me, whichever one I had most need of at the time. So it was that the meeting of Ulysses and Naussica on that beach, the wedding of Jason and Medea in that temple, were the particular cardboard scenes into which I most often breathed life. They were, you could say, my way of ignoring the shortening arcs described daily by the pendulum of our marriage.

Now the worn schoolbook lies open before me again.

... And Jason and Medea came then to the Island in the north, where stood the Temple of Apollo. In that holy place, their hands were joined according to the Rites, and all drank at the Spring of Kardaki. Setting forth to Corinth, it happened that the ship was pursued by Aetes, King of Colchis, father to Medea. But Medea, knowing that the King could not withold proper burial from a son, scattered her brother's limbs upon the sea. And so the Argus passed safely from that place. Fair winds drove the

ship at speed to Corinth, and there Jason did receive the crown of kingship, with all due solemnities. Thereafter, he hastened in secret to take to him the Princess Glauce as his bride ....

But, I wonder as I look away from the page, had Jason never threaded together that series of events: the betrayed father, the murdered brother? Even allowing that this adventurer, in his mad quest for heroism, would have stepped willingly over the bodies of a thousand to reach the Fleece, was there no unease at her tricks with the trade winds, her insistence on the drink at the spring, her chariot always pulled by dragon-serpents?

Alas, no: it seems that those who have their hearts fixed on destiny do not notice what is actually happening in the real world. The book does not speak of how long a time it took for Jason to see Medea clearly; and by then they were both dethroned exiles, sundered wanderers to the ends of that azure sea. Jason, struck down so soon after Corinth and happiness, never saw Medea again: as befitted a sailor, he was killed by a falling timber of the tired ship he had driven too far. The words of the legend before me say that Medea lives on still, flitting harmlessly through the twilight half-life of sleeping minds. And all in vain. To have remembered the source from which their wedding cup was filled, to have heeded the call of the past in time, was that too much for heroes?

'I want to know,' he said, 'I want to know what you're hiding, what happened on this island twenty-five years ago.'

So it begins once more, the recording clicking on in my head, whenever I stop running, forced by exhaustion to think things out, to look again at an old book. It is as if the soundtrack is accompanied by a projector: the kitchen where I sit flickers and fades into grey and white, the hotel bedroom on our last night blooms into focus. The backdrop is a careful arrangement of unmade beds, a suitcase half-packed, clothes thrown over chairs. We are the only actors present on-stage, the others are ghosts evoked by our conversation, since we do not possess sufficient bodies or costumes.

'Spiro, always Spiro,' he says to me, beginning it as I shut the door on the curious lobby, the sideways-glancing corridor. Our arriving draught caught the curtain and it billowed sharply into the room, then hung slackly again. I, too, must have drunk too much, or perhaps it was the storm gathering outside; for a moment the empty balcony was filled with undulating forms.

'You drank too much of that wine', I said, 'he brought us the cheaper one by mistake.'

'Of course. You and Spiro. You want me drunk. So that I can't — can't — .'

75

He began to cry then, and I went into the bathroom for water and a towel, drinking from the glass until the coolness flowed through my veins and I shivered, feeling calmness return.

When I re-entered the room, he was sitting upright on the far bed, his face drying quickly in the night's warmth.

'It was him, wasn't it, all those years ago?' His voice was frantic, but his eyes, turning towards the wall where a single ant hung immobile, did not alter.

'What?' I reached over him to brush the insect down to oblivion, but he caught my wrist and raised it so that I could not move. The fumes of his breath made me reel and I spoke without thinking, wanting only release from the rigid balance of my limbs.

'You're mad,' I said, and heard the words ring out in the lull of the storm.

'Yes, I suppose I am.' There was utter calmness in his tone now, but I was still pinned against the bed, my knees aching from the unyielding stone floor. Then he sighed once, and released me.

'I want to know,' he said again.

'Nothing happened,' I said, but it was no longer true. The wrenching of my muscles had burst the inner core of my memory, and it was all spilling out now into my mouth, almost choking me. The feeling of loss hit me again, as it had done each night of that fortnight when I sat partnerless in the taverna until the very last moment possible, just before the others might flop back down beside me and remark on it. But no matter how long I waited, I always had to join hands with someone who was never the rosy-lipped god I dreamed of, and smile into his face as we whirled around the floor.

'Please,' he said, disgust slurring his voice, 'all of it.'

I rubbed my wrists and sat on the far bed, waiting for him to look at me, but he would not. The tears rolled down my face and fell on my hands, pushing him back behind the misty curtain. I was driven to prevaricate, to tell him a story which might make him give up the hunt. Perhaps then I would be left in peace with my memories. Why, after all, did I not tell him the truth? I ask myself this question again and again; but I could never have explained what was not meant to be fully understood, the way that the spring had captured me so long ago with its yearning song, and filled my vision with the dancing of the maenads, my ears with the smooth unpouring of libations onto the cracked earth.

'All right — if you really want to know — all of it was this. We would stay on in the taverna after our meal and I would dance there with a young man, a student, called Spiro.'

'Spiro. Go on.'

I did not speak for a moment, hardly able to continue with the charade.

'And? You mean that's it?'

'Yes,' I said, thinking of how Spiro's eyes had narrowed as he danced, the way that his arms had lifted us one by one from our feet and spun us around, above the crowd, beneath the vine-covered trellis of the taverna. The others became breathless, they fell to the benches along the walls and were laughing, pointing ....

Spiro had been a nice boy, so polite; he had been almost impartial, perhaps slightly more attentive to Alison. I suddenly remembered her face, and how her tan was streaked with tears as we passed through the boarding gate and began the walk over to the plane.

He was speaking again, jerkily, as he turned his body towards the wall. I wanted to hold him, to wrench him back from the lonely path he had chosen, but he went on turning away and stared at the wall again, where the ant made orderly progress along a downward route. The light bulb flickered and went out, and I could see him only in the flashes of lightning again exploding around us.

'What did he do to you?' he said.

'What do you mean?' I was sorry I had said anything at all. My memories were breaking beneath the burden of my lies, the old misery returning. I inhaled desperately once more the fading sweetness of crushed myrtle and rosemary, straining to hear once more the tiny gurgle of the spring in the early morning air.

'Come on. There must have been something, I know there was.'

'Nothing.' I could hear the pitch of my voice rising, and I wondered why, until now, I had felt compassion.

'Oh, it's all coming out in the wash, isn't it?'

'If that's what you think,' I said.

'You know, of course, that you try to kill everything you touch,' he said, 'me, Danny ....' His voice was slow but strong, the old authority returning.

As I sat on my bed in the dark, I knew I must leave him at that moment, must vanish into the groves of the island among the great trees which each summer continued to give of their fruits in memory of the first spring blossoming. It was an instant of vision worthy of the sybils, but like them I was bound to inaction, the decoding of the message for others my only relief.

Now, as I sit here in the late afternoon of mid-autumn, I look up from the old school primer and see that the leaves are turning vibrantly in the wind, not yet withered or fallen, and I wonder if I can ever break free of destiny and come back to him. He lies, staring upward, on the sofa within a few inches of my fingers' reach; but for him, I am not present. I know this from the paper he throws beneath the table each evening; not alone from the words on the pages whose intermittent sense I can barely decipher, but from the scattering itself. In his wholeness, he would never have untidied his life in my presence, but now his empty thoughts tell him that I am no longer here. I am always on the island.

I wish I knew what legend it was which betrayed him, whispering to him that I would go and never return. I only know of tales which weave more uncertain outcomes, an endless voyage of heroes across the oceans, a ceaseless murmur of waves which reaches me here in this room. When we came home, I took him down to the sea, guiding his steps across the ribbed sand to the edge of the tide. He walked with me through the dry foreshore, but turned away from the water itself, leaning heavily on my arm until I took pity and guided him back.

I set aside the legends and take up instead his ream of notes for today. His eyes are shut; he may be sleeping at last, driven as he is from room to room during the lengthening darkness of evening and night. The rain begins to drip against the window as I shuffle paper, and the trees darken. His words stretch across the width of the page, striving forward to reach the end; the same words, over and over again. I know that he is searching for the way back, but he cannot see my hand when I reach out to him.

Bringing him back to this house was not as difficult as I thought it would be at first, when dawn showed me his immobile limbs, his face still turned against the wall. He was not asleep: when I began to pack, he turned his head and his eyes followed me occasionally, and he dressed himself when I placed his travelling clothes on the bed.

After I had tried to explain to the courier, she looked away from us and walked over to the airport official at the boarding gate. But she need not have worried. They were very kind, putting us among the empty rows at the back where a steward kept bobbing his head between the seats to check that he had not undone his belt or tried to move into the aisle.

'We're fine,' I kept saying as I fended off the offers of blankets, cups of tea, even a brandy. The steward addressed all his remarks to me. Perhaps he had been told that I was the one in need of attention; and perhaps it was so. Certainly, he seemed content, more lively as we approached the end of the flight, nodding and smiling at the curious glances of the other passengers when they walked past our seats, some more often than necessary, it seemed.

I had thought that the aerial map of the city and the bay, tidy and precise as we circled for the last descent, might bring him back. At times, I had hoped never to see this view again; now, I spoke of it unceasingly.

'Look, down there — the city! See — the power station, the river, the mountains ....'

But he only looked down once, and then back into my face, inches away from his, as if puzzled. Once, he reached out to my arm as if to brush something away, but before I could stop myself I had jerked back into my seat and his gesture was arrested, his hand left swinging from his wrist until I placed it back on the armrest.

I have brought him to the specialists, and they have looked at his body and his mind. They use words lightly, like 'trauma' or 'therapy' or 'amnesia', and peer inquisitively at me when I collect him, so that I wonder what new legend he has woven for them.

Danny has come and gone, accusation in his tone as he excused himself from blame. Seeing him crouched on the rug before the fire again made me hunt out the photo albums, but they remained unopened on the table near the sofa, while Danny radiated disapproval.

Writing to Danny was a mistake, I see that now. None of us seemed to recognise each other. He saw Danny as someone from the office and kept up a barrage of neutral, obsequious small talk about things which Danny could not understand: the nameplates on the upper floors, the types of plants which might flourish in the climate of a small office. I watched Danny nod and look sideways. In the kitchen, I tried to tell him about the hierarchy, the pressure that there had been, the kindness of others; but Danny was unimpressed by the video and refused to hear the details I had gathered over the years.

As we drove him to the airport, Danny was stern beside me in the passenger seat, and I made several foolish errors with gears and indicators. I felt an oddly connubial dislike of him, old relationships melting, the other in the back seat the only strained link holding my son to me. By the time we arrived at the departure lounge, I almost expected Danny to pat him on the head and give me custody of a package of expensive confectionery. But there was no parting gift, only promises.

'I'll be back with Miranda as soon as I can. Try not to worry yourself — I'm sure that things will ... work out. Soon.'

'We'll be fine,' I said, 'don't worry.'

'I hope you have a productive trip', he said then, lurching forward eagerly from my side, 'everything will be taken care of while you're away. I'll make sure to water the plants — the upper offices can get very warm if the heating is on at this season.'

Danny was silent, his head bowed, but I did not want to help him. We stood there, each of us staring into our separate mirrors, until the announcement was made and Danny could escape.

'Bastard,' he said as we waved at the shoulders in the crowded distance, 'you heard, of course, what he did last week to O'Grady?'

'Yes, dear, mind the revolving door,' I said, and he lapsed into almost inaudible muttering as we skirted the taxi rank, so that no one noticed.

The leaves will begin to fall soon under the weight of the rain: already their branches are sluggish in the wind. It rains on the island all winter, they say, the constant clouds unpouring their gift onto the rock and clay which store it for the hot spring and summer, keeping the garden fresh under months of searing skies.

As he begins to snore, I gather up the rest of his pages and clip them together, ready for his next visit to the hospital. If they agree, I will take him back there next spring, to where it all fell asunder, to retrack past the point of no return. If he would only take my hand, I know that this time I would have the courage to lead him onward the full way, past the fragrant banks of thyme and myrtle. I might even have strength enough for both, and we might find each other again, there where the rosemary blooms: pungent oils for my phial to jog the memory. Tiny blue flowers and spears of dark green: "rosemary, that's for remembrance". It was always one of my favourite herbs, my most often thought of quotation, and now I cannot get it out of my head.

Then, as I look down at him sleeping, arms folded stiffly around his waist as if to imitate a dead hero's tomb, I wonder if he would ever dare to tread the sacred paths a second time. He is, after all, no Jason, and I had never meant to be Medea. But as my thoughts fail in the twilight silence, I am drawn in to the steadying beat of my heart. It tells me not to falter, not to believe that remembrance exists only because of the past, an act concluded, and that legends never end.

The Pear Tree

The pear tree in my father's garden was shelter to my childhood. As soon as I was old enough, I would use its cover to pull myself up the wall, stone by crumbling stone, until I could look over into the lost domain of next door. As my eyes rose above the edge, the imagined laughter and rustling of newspapers which had lured me from the house were transformed into sunhats, a deckchair, a low table with an upturned book. It did not really matter that there was no one in the deckchair: the rampant lawn and crouching trees told me enough; even then, prescient, I was learning to distil clues from objects, ignoring voices. Next door was a different continent to the desert on which my toes dangled, back to which my aching shoulders were dropping me. Afterwards, I would scarcely notice the leaves of skin frayed from my wrists, the rawness of my knee, overcome as I was by my vision.

I have long forgotten who those neighbours were, what they looked like; but the memory of their garden has stayed with me always. Later on, I came to need that memory more; now, in this flat where I have come to wait out my old age, I seem to need it most of all.

'Hello there,' she would always begin, the woman who lived downstairs.

'Good morning,' I replied.

'Terrible the way the grass grows this weather.'

'Is it?' I said, usually to myself, when I had reached the landing in front of my flat; sometimes, I glanced back over the banisters to where she still lingered, half turned towards her kitchen, a wet or floury hand plucking at the pocket of her smart apron.

The exchange never varied, which was why, as my world grew more silent, its voices distant, then blurred, I shunned others' conversation and sought hers. There was no need to read her lips: our exchanges were rehearsed and immutable.

Except once, when, as I crossed the hall, she burst out of her door more suddenly than usual, her untied apron tangling her stride. She looked into my face carefully.

'Would you ever mind — you're going down to the post office today aren't you — dropping this in the box? I wouldn't ask you, but I can't go out just now.'

As she shut the door quickly, I thought I glimpsed him advancing behind her, his hand grasping furiously for something just lost. The envelope, damp in one corner where she had held it, bore the name 'Liam Lally'. All those labials: the most difficult to decipher; I remember it because of my relief she hadn't spoken the name.

From March until September — sometimes October — I watched fascinated as her husband continually mowed the grass. He was as obessional as my father had been, in another garden, far away from here; long ago. Week after week, the whirr of his motor had followed me through the pages of Ellery Queen, while my homework waited uneasily nearby on the diningroom floor. 'My father's garden,' I always call it, since my mother never entered it, unless to put the washing on the line which divided it exactly down the middle. As she struggled on frosty mornings with the stiff pegs, the shrubs marched down the walls to the privet hedge at the bottom, two by resigned two, facing each other across the grass and the thin strips of concrete separating them.

'Forsythia, hypericum, escallonia.' He would count them aloud every evening as though afraid one might escape if not watched. The shrubs were clipped small, each in its plot; any leaflet which had uncurled was snipped away at the next evening inspection.

Only the pear tree disturbed the symmetry: old and gnarled and branching, it reared up above the bowed heads of the other plants. Our house was then some thirty years old, but it seemed to me the tree was so twisted, its bark so worn, that it must have stood in the same spot long before the estate went up. In my father's garden, it was like the reproachful ghost of acres of lush, forgotten orchards. If it had not been for my mother's zeal to preserve its uncompromising barrenness, her crusade of stolid mealtime silences when I clattered my knife and fork between them for company, it would never have survived as long as it did. It still stood all the time of my adolescence; but when I came away from the house after my mother's funeral and sat grieving in the flat, the significance of the changed view from my old bedroom window slowly became clear to me. I knew then that I had no longer any reason for homesickness.

When I first moved here after my retirement, I looked out of my top-floor window, and I felt that fear again. Expectantly raising my binoculars, I began to read the story of this new garden, realising that it was probably the last time I would make such a beginning. Then I saw that all was being obliterated; scarcely a trace of its past remained.

For the past year, a vast green sward has steadily marched from the back wall to the cement paving below my window; one by one, he has dug up the shrubs along the wall, the rose-beds scattered across the lawn; usually in spring, when the tips of the bushes are soft and green. Once, a rose was actually in flower when he brutalised it, scattering orange petals on the bare earth. He is strangely careful, then, when sowing the grass seed, mixing the chaff with sand before he swings his arm back and forth in a steady rhythm, the brim of his gardening hat swaying. There is something evil about this methodical levelling.

For relief, I have sometimes aimed the glasses at next door, although the overgrown bushes along their wall impede my view. A young couple have apparently been refurbishing the house, ripping out tawdry partitions, rotten floorboards, ancient rubbish, to end up in the skip outside their front door. But, in the garden, they seem content to let things recover their old ways.

How often have I watched the young man reclaiming the flower beds from the incursions of grass, upturning the most stubborn clods to the winter frost; all last winter they lay there, the underbelly of the turf thrust up at the sky, the hidden green carpet becoming matted yellow, then rotted, until he re-emerged last month, shrugging his anorak onto his shoulders. At the first pound of his spade, the sods collapsed, one by defenceless one, porous from weeks of icy nights.

'We'll plant apple trees there in the autumn,' said the young women one sharp bright day, pointing to the end of the garden. Her face was turned up towards her lover as she spoke; I could not see what he said, but he grabbed her suddenly, then chased her round the corner of the lawn, out of my range of vision. All at once, it was as if I were young again, in the centre of things, meeting new people, still believing in myself. The next day, I was over my joy: such things are foolishness, after all.

In this garden, the man works alone, bending away from me to pull the starter of the mower or to neaten further the perfectly straight edges of the lawn, so that I rarely see his expression. I can tell nothing about this couple who live feet below me from the movements they make in the garden: they never sit in deckchairs on the terrace, or talk outside — she ventures out only to summon him to meals. 'Tea's ready,' she calls, I imagine, over the roar of the motor or the thumping of the spade. He never replies, but she does not seem to expect it, walking slowly back to the house. It will be some time later before he follows, brisk, meticulous in removing the tools of his work as he goes.

Some weeks ago, as I watched him cut down the last tree, I thought I would fall from the chair with sadness. It too was a pear tree; the shelter of my childhood trembled as he raised the hatchet triumphantly. When I could bring myself to return to the window, I saw that he had abandoned the small, black tear in the turf which was the roots' final protest. Its horror circled my heart and I could not sleep for many nights, blinking in the darkness until the flashes behind my eyes became the rays of the dawn sun slicing their way through the curtains of my room. All one night, the house trembled in outrage, strange vibrations jarring my cheek on the pillow. At last, I was driven to raise my head and strain into the darkness, rigid with terror: but there was nothing, and I sobbed for my impotence.

Things have not been the same since then: the silence from outside is absolute, but there is a strange ringing in my ears, a jangling which becomes persistent towards evening. Perhaps it is a physical manifestation of my uncertainty: sitting over the acrid fumes of my gas fire as the twilight circles outside the window, it is hard to imagine that there is anything beyond the walls of my room and the possessions whose shadowy outlines mock me. I no longer go out, fearing to meet him; although, once, I forced myself to go shopping, just to cross the hall and meet the woman again, to resume the old, redundant, lifesaving ritual. But she has not appeared for some time and I feel bereaved, as if for a parent, cherishing the secret of the letter we once shared. He, on the other hand, is still here: but, on the few occasions when I could not avoid him, he turned away and mumbled quickly because he knew I could not understand, mockery shining from his eyes as he turned back to stare at me.

My few books are in a heap at the foot of the bookcase; I can no longer find an order for them on the shelves, much less make sense of their pages. As I struggle to decode the flickering blue images of my television, I wonder why she has gone, whether the one incident between them in the garden which I observed was somehow linked to the felling of the pear tree, or simply the culmination of their secret life.

'Bitch.' He was screaming at her, for once not trying to maintain his mask. This time, I could make out everything that he said, although, after a moment, I wished I could not. I sensed her fear, even though her back was towards me as she stood there, hiding the gap left by the pear tree, clutching for the paper he flicked just outside her reach. Then he taunted her with a name, a name which teased at the edge of my memory — but perhaps I was mistaken, labials are always the most difficult to see clearly, the hardest to remember.

That is always the problem: I can remember nothing clearly any more. 'Have you noticed anything suspicious?' they asked, those nice men who would not have a cup of tea. 'Were there signs of a struggle?' they asked then, after I had told them what I thought, repeating the question until I understood, so patient. But, when I spoke of vibrations, they glanced at one another.

'I know,' I said, 'vibrations are not sounds; but often sounds may not even be sign enough. Sometimes, if you look into a person's garden,' I said, 'even if the garden is empty, you can know a lot of things'. But I could not explain my intuitions; as to what I have seen, there is nothing after all, so extraordinary in a quarrel. So, they would not come to look out into the garden, but eased themselves from the flat as I stood by the window, trying not to hurt my feelings.

I suppose he must have reported her missing: he is quite safe — I learned that from the mechanical tone of their questions, the fact that they have not come back. The last time I saw him was just after she ... left. Out in the garden, sowing the final plot of grass. I did not watch him for long. Lately, I have sensed a disturbance in my room, not discernible among the jumble of my possessions, but from a slight alien odour mingling with the gas fumes when I returned from my bath. Perhaps I should look out again while there is still time. He might not disturb the garden further, since there is nothing left for him to destroy. It is almost peaceful now, beginning to establish its own continuity; if I have long enough here, there might be daisies in the lawn, even a stray flowerseed borne in by the wind. This warm spring has encouraged growth: if next year's is as good, there may be blossoms on the apple trees next door. The pear tree's grave must already have greened: soon there will be no sign of disturbance and the rustle of its leaves will be only a vibration in my ears, no more real than the footsteps I imagine are climbing the stairs, no more believable than an old woman's ramblings.

But, look: focusing the glasses once more on the lawn, fine tuning the lenses, I can see that the garden still, for a short while, honours the pear tree's memory: in a strangely large space where the tree's roots once lay, the new grass shows up from above as a paler green, the fragile spikes sketching an oblong shape.

DIARY FROM A HOUSE CALLED
'THE WOLF FOLD'

In the spare bedroom, kneeling in front of a shabby suitcase, the woman fumbled desperately through the tumbled belongings that were not her own, searching for some tiny thing to alleviate guilt. She came across a diary, a thin cardboard notebook, scarcely worth the title scrawled on its cover. But she removed it from the heap, turned the flimsy pages — and started at the childishness of the girl's handwriting, sure that she herself had never half-made her letters in that careless way, even as a young girl. She suddenly realised how differently she and the girl must have been formed: countries apart, classes divergent, generations separate.

She stared for a moment, unseeingly, at the open page and then began to read the first diary entry:

Long and very winding road from the station to the village. Glad to climb out into the cold mountain air. Nobody much around at 7.30 in the morning. Then a car pulled up — it was Madame. She seems okay, very chic, a bit 'stiff upper lip' the way they all are. I must see if I can pick up some fashion hints from her.

The short drive to the chalet is very spectacular. I suppose people living here must get used to it — Madame started looking at me as if I had two heads when I asked if there were any wolves left — after all, the house is called 'La Combe aux Loups', which means 'the wolf fold', and a dark and dense looking wood almost crowds it off the mountain. Hope Monsieur and the baby are a bit more friendly. Must get down to unpacking, etc.

Yes, the road was spectacular between Sallanches and the village. But there was also the feeling of loneliness when you looked up at the sheer valley walls which held no blade of grass, even in midsummer; the cruelty of it did not diminish with familiarity. On her many trips from the city, the bus driver would protectively stack the only other passenger — the daily newspapers — behind his seat. He never made any response to conversation, so that, after a while, she began to sit halfway down the empty bus. At unpredictable intervals on the road, the driver would leap down from his perch to deliver segments of the wedge of papers to tiny hamlets flung into crevices of the mountain; she watched on each occasion the same mime of welcome and then somehow poignant farewell as the bus pulled away ruthlessly up the steep road. The feeling that she was not really present on the bus, that passengers were not necessary for it to continue to ply its route, grew stronger with each trip. The driver's only glances backward were for the safety of his papers as his bus slithered round ten kilometres of hairpin bends between the niched villages.

The pages of the diary crackled as she turned them further. A musty smell sprang out as a tiny withered flower slipped down onto the fireplace. Already, she sensed that the relief she sought was not to be found here — even, that she might find out things that she did not want to know — yet she was compelled to continue. She reached down without looking and threw the remains of the flower into the embers as she went on reading.

19 September

The weather has been glorious all the week I've been here. When I take the baby for a walk I can hear only the clanging of cowbells which could be a mile away. There are very few signs of habitation — only now and again a black speck on the meadows which might be a farmer at work. For a moment, I could feel like Dorothy Wordsworth when William sat with her above Tintern Abbey... yet here there are not even ruins or smoke from chimneys to show the presence of human beings. If it was only like this everywhere, just animals and trees, it would indeed be a brave, new world. But good old W.W. had to drum up such an interest in Nature (with a capital N, of course) that it all got spoiled. If I was Dorothy, I couldn't have stood his goody-goodiness about man and nature very long without murdering him!

23 September

It's raining today: so much for Mother Nature. At least that horrible gloomy forest is now invisible — I miss the grandeur of Mont Blanc, though. The mist dripping off the end of my nose in the garden is making me homesick.

Madame looks at me strangely when I try to talk to her — very intensely, answering my attempts at chat in monosyllables. The only subject she shows any interest in is the baby's routine — and that's somewhat limited. I'm beginning to feel frustrated for want of communication. We haven't seen much of Paul who's away on business somewhere, but he seemed more friendly than his wife.

It was harder to read the last sentences, but she did not move to turn on the lamp. She let the diary fall to her lap as she looked into her own memory of the weather that early autumn: there had been afternoons of brilliant sunshine as well as rain, days when she wandered, mostly with the baby, sometimes on her own, across the pasture above the cottage. Sitting in a hollow, she looked down the miles of open valley, lush grassland sprawled in the dark yellow sunlight; in her city-bred youth she had never imagined such panoramas. Now, it all belonged to her: the wind waving the greenness was hers, the baby was hers. She would gaze down on him as he lay moving his limbs tentatively, perfect round blue eyes blinking up from the shade of the white sunhat, and grab him to her so violently that sometimes she was afraid she would harm him. He was hers; she would not give him over to anyone else.

As soon as the girl arrived, she had seen at once that she was not passive like the young servants she employed in Paris: this one was seeking something. At first, she had thought it was the baby and she spent a lot of time with the two of them, watching. It was not long before it dawned on her that the baby was safe, that the girl had barely a professional interest in him; she knew then that it had to be Paul. As soon as she realised this, she could feel her lifelong control, the discipline, slipping away. She began, for the first time in her life, to suffer frequent headaches; nightmares woke her often.

The most abiding of her nightmares began the way the others had, with the feeling of shame, the need to run away, but that was not all. There was more detail, familiar yet horribly uncomforting. She stood in the main room of what seemed to be her parents' home, facing the rest of her family across the dining-table. They stared; whether with accusation or some other emotion it was impossible to discover: her vision was becoming distorted, she saw their figures elongate and the tops of their heads curve in towards the fireplace, as through the thick glass at the bottom of a tumbler. She could not know what she had done to provoke their gaze, their alien censoring. Suddenly, in her dream, the walls began to heave and crumble inwards. She did not feel terror yet, only a severe sense of puzzlement, so that she was able to turn and run between the gaping bricks, leaving her unbelonging relatives to the holocaust. Relieved to be free, she ran up the steep pasture: to avoid the precipices, upwards to the trees. They closed behind her with a clanging noise like lift doors. A phrase she had heard applied to ailing childhood pets rang in her ears, 'better put out of its misery quickly,' and with it the same sickening lurch at her heart. There was just enough light in the forest to hint at the outlines of pits underfoot. And now, something followed her. The terror began, it crept up from her feet, slowly but not slowly enough, clamping her muscles into inaction. She knew she must turn, she knew she must kill first, she knew she must turn ....

'Paul!' She sat up in bed, but her imagined shout must have been silent; he did not shift in his cocoon of blankets. A cloying dawn mist blotted out the light from the windows; she heard the muffled crack of the hunters' bullets from the mountain top.

The next night, she hurried early to bed, hoping to escape from the sleep cycle of the previous weeks. She drank a brandy and dozed after an eternity of willpower. Almost immediately, it seemed, that a scream woke her, and pounded on and on as she jumped into a robe and ran to the baby's room. By the time she arrived, the baby was quietened and the room had filled with other comforters. 'There was no need to disturb yourself,' Paul said, 'it was only a nightmare.' The baby, rocked in his arms, obediently dozed. The other was also there, in a corner by the cot, smiling encouragement at Paul's suggestion that the two 'girls' go back to bed, an odd term — now, she recognised it as a diary password.

She left the room without waiting to see if the other was following and padded quickly down the corridor, dodging the flickering pits of shadow on the floorboards, painful to look at in the moonlight, its daytime friendliness vanished. She was still afraid to look round, but no sound of footsteps followed.

Rubbing her feet under chill sheets, she tried to relax, but was compelled to listen for the sound of their return to bed. The scene in the baby's room was etched in bold outline on the wall of the bedroom. She imagined her mother and father looking on, but she could not erase her shame. She had not often seen him so, naked in spirit as well as in body; and he had held the baby in proud male domination of the madonna, her role. He had seemed unknowable to her in that crouching stance, his clothed vulnerability become angular bones. The shadow he had thrown on the lamplit wall had been huge, violent, enthralling the baby, extinguishing her. Meanwhile, the other's smile gleamed from the shadow triumphantly.

Despite her anxiety, perhaps because of it, she fell into a dark, dreamless well; when she woke, Paul had already left for work and his pillow was chill. She could not remember if he had come back to bed or not ....

The fire in the room had nearly gone out, but she felt herself approaching an ending of sorts. Skipping the next few paragraphs, which were to her uninteresting, she read:

I've been getting out and about a bit now that the rain's stopped. I met the farmer beside the chalet — it's peculiar to hear him, he speaks in proverbs about everything — the crops, the weather, the animals. Those sayings are his Ten Commandments. He even believes that there's an afterlife for animals and that he will meet his dog in the Hereafter. It's an oddly primitive culture here — the small parish church, the blow-in, has been shut up ever since I arrived, with a large padlock fastened to the grill through which all the dead leaves drift into the aisles...

She looked away from the page with pain, remembering the day they had met the farmer with the brown haired collie. The dog fawned on his master, who tickled its head with a twig.

After the quarrel, Paul had gone away — for a few days, forever, she did not know. From then on, she could not let the girl out of her sight, tracking her everywhere, even on the strolls she took with the baby. She could sense the girl's discomfort as they walked in silence across the valley. As the farmer and the girl had spoken, she had watched, smiling at the girl's unease, the sense of loneliness that she experienced in her dreams vanishing at last: here was a kindred fear, a sister anxiety she had been able to provoke.

'Yes, yes,' the farmer was gesturing irritably, 'he's a killer; my neighbours have dead sheep to prove it. I must shoot him tomorrow early.'

As she smiled on, the idea began to hover on the fringes of vision, then hit her suddenly like a blow to the chest. The girl continued to plead for the dog's life.

'But mightn't it be something else, I don't know, wolves or something?'

'Wolves!' The farmer pushed his cap back from his forehead and re-adjusted it forward again, snorting with laughter. 'Pepe is not a wolf, but he's no use with sheep now. He must be put down.' He turned away sadly towards her own rictus grin as he continued — but he could hardly know how each word thumped like a mallet against her heart.

'I will shoot him tomorrow in the forest at dawn.'

Yes. Something spoke the word behind her voice, behind her mind. The farmer was answering the other's question as he turned away, impatient at this interruption to the natural course of events:

'Up there, because — I can't shoot him in sight of the pasture where I trained him.'

The last diary entry now. She was weary as she read it, so tired and dizzy that she could barely make out some of the scrawled letters, the foreign thought.

I can't believe that anyone would shoot that beautiful young dog. I can't argue with them. He just keeps saying that 'Pepe will go straight up There' and points in the direction of Mont Blanc. Why all those Romantic poets thought that mountain was uplifting, I don't know. It leans, it threatens, all the time. You can't look at anything else without it creeping back into the corner of your eye.

I'm alone here now with the baby and Madame. Paul left late one night. I have no-one to talk to; I don't know her at all. I heard them shouting in the night before Paul left. I feel a lot more than a thousand miles away from home whenever she looks at me with those deep black eyes. She won't say anything, won't even answer me about the dog. I'm beginning to be afraid here. Maybe I was too friendly with Paul — and that night in the baby's room — perhaps she got some idea then ... oh, I don't know.

(Later)

I've decided to follow the farmer into the forest tomorrow and try to stop him. Maybe I could argue with him, distract him, let Pepe go free ... I've just told Madame, she actually showed some kind of agreement.

Wrote my first poem ever (maybe the last!) at dawn yesterday. It was after a frightening dream where I fell. When a shot woke me I was shaking. It was only the early hunters, of course, there are so many of them; even Paul has a gun which he uses sometimes, so he told me, for rabbits. I thought of wild animals, say wolves — and wrote this ....

The woman shivered violently as she saw that the lines of the poem (it had been quite short) had been completely obliterated. She closed the diary and placed it on top of the clothes in the suitcase beside her, fastened the lid, or began to, and stopped. After a long time, while the dusk crept further outwards from the corners of the room and her hands remained frozen on the case, she stirred and reopened the locks. Taking up her notepad and pen, she wrote to the other mother her sorrow at her daughter's untimely death, such an unfortunate accident ... so many such tragedies during this season. Though she wrote as hard and as fast as she could, she could not unclench her teeth in remembrance of gulped breath, the unaccustomed weight of the gun, foxholes. It had been an endless stumbling after the flash of white until she heard the shots from in front of both of them, saw the girl stop dead at the sound and could line up the back of her head in the sights ... just more stumbling after that, the feeling of shame gone at last, until she saw in safety from her home the farmer come running in terror from the trees ....

She underlined her signature viciously and folded the sheet without care, pushing it down the side of the clothes. She hesitated a moment before she took the diary from the case and threw it onto the fire where it took a long time to burn. There was no question of it, the girl's guilt had been clear from the text; she had broken and entered the chalet with her mind; only now was the world safe again.

After she had reduced the ashes to an unobtrusive layer in the grate, she joined Paul on the terrace to watch the sunset bloody the peaks. The smell of burnt paper clinging to her fingers was the suspended sadness of early autumn, the oblique rays of the sun fragmented by mountain crests; frosted mornings and icy nights. She thought of a view from the top window of the chalet in the early half light of a distant, much lower valley whose steel-girdered bridge already caught the full morning sun; in the evening, the sun still blazing on the *arrêt* long after the chalet was plunged into twilight; at night, rocking the baby to sleep, the feeling of being a last survivor, waiting for the fringe of the holocaust to curl around her ankles.

The new maid moved quietly onto the terrace.

'Shall I feed the baby now, Madame?'

Looking round sharply, she was relieved to see that the girl's gaze was cast down listlessly — but then she raised her eyes slowly and looked full ahead. It became obvious then that the girl had deep, black eyes into which the light of the setting sun sank without trace: shameful eyes.

THE FREE DAY

On Thursday afternoon they lounged as usual in Mary's kit-chen, feet planted in the small patches of sunlight which warmed the black and white tiles. Mary lifted the teapot ex-perimentally, then without asking poured the last of the darkened tea into the two mugs in equal measure. As she replaced the pot on its stand, Mairin began screaming outside in short breathless bursts. Although Mary seemed not to notice, Hannah couldn't help glancing past the net curtain to make sure Tomo was all right. As she half-expected, Mairin was merely screaming in delighted terror as she fled down the unkempt lawn, her brother Ciaran's cupped hands thrusting forward some horrible thing dug from the rockery. Tomo sat happily on his own, alternately chewing one of his building blocks and trying to force it between Blackie's unthreatening jaws. Hannah sank back again in the comfortable chair and tried to shake off the feeling of being at the dentist; nausea gripped her as she smelled the strong tea.

It was almost a year ago exactly that Mary had come up with the idea of the free day. During one of these same sessions, they had talked about the short-comings of babysitters and remarked on how lucky they were to have each other, only ten doors apart, to step in whenever needed. It was only really necessary to get a babysitter when the four of them, Hannah and Adrian, Mary and Harry, went out together, for the autumn dinner-dance or the Christmas show at McConnell Transit. These evenings, despite the logistics of getting someone to mind the three children, were a great success. Nonetheless, Mary said, it was important for the two of them to keep up their own interests, not to become bogged down at home. Hannah had agreed totally, without really being sure of what Mary meant. So, for the past year, they had minded each other's children on alternate Fridays, organising school, meals and whatever appointments with the doctor could not be rearranged; nothing must be allowed to interfere with the free day.

'Well, where are you off to tomorrow?' As Hannah opened her mouth to answer, Mary leaped up and ran out to chastise Ciaran, who was now trying to get Tomo to look at and, inevitably, eat his latest specimen. Hannah thought again about the chronology of events she had narrated to Mary two weeks ago. To sustain themselves over a fortnight, Mary had stipulated the one condition that they must each relate in detail their adventures; the debriefing, they called it. In the few seconds while she watched Mary seize Ciaran by the back of his jersey, cuff him on the leg and shove him away from Tomo, Hannah struggled to remember the diary of events which she typed out painstakingly every second week and which she kept in a folder under her side of the bed.

On the first Friday morning, almost a year ago, Hannah had eagerly hurried down the empty road from Mary's house towards the bus stop, almost ready to sprint if any of the neighbours had appeared in front of her. Luckily, it was almost ten o'clock, the hour when the saloon cars had all departed for town, when children had long been ferried to school and front doors were shut on scenes involving overloaded washing machines and tangled vacuum flexes: Hannah recognised the vibrations of effort which emanated from the houses, since the same pattern formed her own mid-mornings. Only the few like Mary would have everything under control and be drinking coffee in company with the Gay Byrne Show.

Still nobody appeared as she progressed down the road. Half an hour later she would have been sure to meet someone struggling to the newsagent-grocery with pram or stubborn toddler determined to investigate every square inch of the pavement.

'Hi, Hannah, how are you?' they would say, unable to hide their surprise that she was child-free. 'Where's Tomo?'

She had her excuses ready, but she was unwilling to destroy the delicate balance of this, the first day, with lies, although she knew she would have to lie to Adrian soon enough. It was understood that the institution of the free day be kept secret from everyone they knew, including Harry and Adrian: that was where the freedom lay, Mary had suggested.

Unaccosted as she reached the corner, Hannah had felt a quick pang as she imagined Tomo alone in Mary's untidy back garden — Harry was not a keen gardener — yelling more and more loudly for her as Mary tried to distract him. Then she recalled Tomo's actual equanimity when left in Mary's care and the time when Mary said apologetically that it came from being one of a large family herself, wiping away with one gesture tears which had been flooding Hannah's lap unstoppably.

The driver meandered in and out of the suburb for several minutes before he reached the main road into town. Still Hannah could not grasp the fact that she was liberated for the day, even though she had climbed upstairs for a treat; she would never have attempted the top deck with Tomo. The neat paths and regimented rose-bushes of the gardens below reminded her of Adrian. If they went out for a drive on Sunday, she often saw him glancing out his side window at the houses they passed, comparing the glimpsed patterns with his own efforts: gardening was Adrian's passion. In fact, Hannah often felt that she shared more in Adrian's working existence than in the life he led in the gardens each evening before the nine o'clock news, changed into old jeans and jumper, while she corralled Tomo in the bathroom, rashly promising stories as she struggled to dry him. After the news, when the volume had been turned down for the advertisements, she and Adrian would discuss endlessly the latest office intrigues and Hannah often caught herself thinking that she was still working in the company.

Such was Hannah's insider feeling for the hierarchic relationships which made up McConnell Transit that she had known, before Adrian actually said so, that Harry's star had been on the wane in recent months, in contrast to Adrian's increasing usefulness to the MD. Why this was so was not explained — 'Harry's got a bit of a chip nowadays,' was all Adrian said — but Hannah felt that an explanation would suggest itself sooner or later, so embroiled was she in the complicities of the management pyramid.

When she had stepped off the bus in town, Hannah automatically turned to catch hold of Tomo's hand, but saw only the conductor helping an elderly woman down from the step. Later, as she struggled through the throngs of foreign students in Bewley's to find a small corner in which to rest her shopping bag — although she had yet failed to track down most of the items on her list — Hannah felt a deep sense of annoyance. She glanced at her watch: if she left straight away, she might just catch the one o'clock bus home.

After that first day, Hannah never went into town at all, spending her free day behind half-closed venetian blinds, terrified that Mary passing might glimpse a movement. She developed a routine of returning to bed with a fat paperback until lunchtime; in the afternoon, she had a long bath with a generous helping of Radox or watched re-runs of films on television, trying to avoid the children's programmes which made her miss Tomo.

Now, as Mary returned from the garden, smiling expectantly, Hannah decided to tell her the truth about her free days. She had been determined for several weeks now, frustration increasing with each passing week. What had prevented her was Mary's eagerness for detail and her excitement, which must surely have given away the secret to Harry and the others, at the approach of her own Friday.

Hannah had begun to write the diary two months ago, as a reminder and guide to the fiction she had spun. At first, she had written herself into a round of cinema going, shopping and crowd-watching from the balcony of Bewley's in Grafton Street. She culled the storylines of the films easily enough from the Sunday papers, but she felt nervous describing the latest shop displays, afraid that Mary on the following Friday would disprove the bargains so casually listed. However, Mary seemed to lack much interest in these things, preferring instead to hear of the people Hannah had encountered during the day. This, and the fact that it was safer to dwell on the fictitious relationships she developed, gave birth to Hannah's admirer.

Essentially, it was a nebulous, romantic liaison, progressing from mild friendship as a result of discussions in Bewley's to — as Hannah became more confident and Mary more avid — a tender, but so far innocent series of meetings at the cinema or for morning coffee. By the time the relationship was two months old, Hannah's script was running into two folders and she had transferred it to a safer location behind the Encyclopaedia Britannica on the bottom shelf of the bookcase in her sittingroom.

Today, her notes were well prepared — they would run to several typed pages when she got round to it next week, she reckoned — and Mary was pink with excitement as she walked her back to her own house, barely in time for tea and Adrian's return.

'It's wonderful the way things worked out for you, Hannah,' Mary murmured wistfully as the gate squeaked. 'Nothing like that will ever happen to me.'

While Hannah had adapted reasonably well to the fiction of her own free day, deriving a certain amount of creative pride from the lines of neat typing which filled her folders, she found Mary's Fridays more and more intolerable. For convenience, she brought Tomo round to Mary's, collecting Mairin from her playgroup at noon and Ciaran from the primary school at two o'clock. Mairin was a quiet enough child on her own and she would play fairly peaceably with Tomo for hours. Without Mary, Ciaran seemed to Hannah to cross the thin line from boisterousness to hyperactivity, and infected the other two with wilfulness. When at lunchtime she watched Tomo being patiently dressed up or down or 'taught' by Mairin, Hannah fondly thought how like a junior Adrian he had become; by mid-afternoon, as she dragged him filthy and roaring with fury from the precarious games Ciaran had invented, she could scarcely recognise him as her own. At five o'clock, when Mary gave her cheerful ring at the door, they were all exhausted, sullenly quiet; but Mary gave no sign of noticing. Even as Hannah hauled Tomo through the door, Ciaran and Mairin were re-emerging as the pleasant, exuberant three- and five-year-olds Mary had left in the morning; and Tomo, waving from Hannah's neck, became once again her own.

'See you on Monday as usual — for the debriefing,' Mary hissed in a stage-whisper as Hannah walked down the road.

It was the rule that only major domestic dramas could interrupt the unfolding of the debriefing: but, no matter how high he climbed among the trees, Ciaran never broke his leg, and Mairin's screams never quite reached the point of self-asphyxiation. So Hannah smilingly listened as Mary told of her cinema visits, her hairdresser's boyfriend problems, the man with dark eyes she had seen on the opposite escalator in Switzers — uneventful days compared with Hannah's, Mary sighed.

Only one significant event ever occurred while Hannah was in Mary's house, but after some thought she decided not to mention the fact that Harry rang looking for Mary almost every second Friday, especially as Harry himself had stressed it was not important. The calls had been going on for a couple of months and at first Hannah had thought that Harry must be trying to make a pass at her, using the opportunity of Mary's absence. When he did not progress from a few jokey remarks of the sort he usually made, she found herself making excuses as best she could — Mary was at the hairdresser, or, he had just missed her, she had gone to the shop. She thought that Harry seemed satisfied at this and put the whole thing to the back of her mind. After all, Mary and Harry probably rang each other every day for all she knew; she and Adrian sometimes had to telephone, although usually they sorted out arrangements over breakfast.

Then, one Friday, just as Hannah was swallowing two aspirin to clear her headache, Harry arrived in the hall. When she said hello, he grinned at her as usual, but in daylight she saw lines along his forehead which had not been visible at the last dinner-dance.

'Bit of a handful, eh?' he said to her in a sympathetic manner when he heard the uproar from the back, but did not otherwise refer to Mary's absence. Perhaps Mary had told him she wouldn't be in, Hannah thought, although she had noticed a flicker of concern cross his face when she emerged from the sitting-room.

'Forgot some papers this morning, you see,' he explained as he opened the sittingroom door. Out of politeness, Hannah went into the kitchen, saying that she was just putting on the kettle if he'd like a quick cup. It was only as the water struck the aluminium with a clang that she remembered she had left her typescript open at the latest entry on the coffee table, where she had been checking over the scenario for next week.

She turned off the tap and listened to the silence in the house. Outside, the children were suspiciously hushed. After a moment, realising that the other two were breathlessly watching Ciaran climb higher than he had ever been before, she turned on the tap again until the kettle was nearly full, banged on the window to let Ciaran know she had seen him, and lit the gas, which flared up with a pop. Just as she was reaching up for two mugs, the front door slammed, so she only made a small pot of tea; her headache was already beginning to clear.

Adrian came in early from the garden the following week while Hannah was still waiting for the news to come on and told her about Harry's sudden transfer to Letterkenny. This was news to Hannah, who had not seen Mary for some days. Nonetheless, as Adrian added, 'Not that it was all that sudden, you know,' she nodded, realising she had known for some time that Harry's slide might accelerate.

Later, as the trailer for tomorrow's scheduled programmes replaced the isobars of the weather forecast, he added, glancing almost accusingly at her, that 'it was Mary's carry-on that did for Harry — but I suppose you knew about all that, you and Mary being such great buddies'.

'I used to babysit for her of course, from time to time,' Hannah replied gently, pausing to check that she had not dropped any stitches of the jersey she was knitting for Tomo, 'but I don't know what you mean by carry-on. She would go shopping, or get her hair done, that's all.'

Adrian gave a single guffaw. As he went out to lock up the lawnmower, he bent down and kissed her, telling her what a little innocent she was; but too many people had known about the thing, it was no use her being loyal.

As they settled down on the sofa waiting for the opening credits of the late film, Hannah said, 'Yes, we'll miss them all right,' and stretched out her bare foot to the bright warmth of the fire. She thought she might take Tomo to the zoo next Friday. Both of them especially loved the sea-lions, hurrying to watch them slipping underwater in their pool and resurfacing suddenly quite close, when you least expected it. Imagining the sequence of cages they would pass on their way to the pool, Hannah felt a twinge from her remote past, the sensation that she was utterly free. It was a feeling from long before childbirth, before marriage, even from beyond the days when she had worked in McCambridge Transit and the future had been bursting with events. Eventually she decided that it had been the same feeling as the day she received the results of her final school exams, and saw the years of closely written copybooks distilled into a few marks on a page. On that day too, she had made a ritual blaze in the fireplace.

THE SOLITARY TRAVELLER

The day was warm and sunny. As he searched for the shop, Mr
Flanagan slipped off his jacket and folded it, sleeves inward,
over his arm. He had spotted the notice last year as the coach
slowed through the narrow town and he found the shop exactly
where he remembered, at the turn for the harbour, the yellowed
paper of the notice still jostling rubber boots and arcane machinery.

'One ticket, please.'

'For the Cape or for Sherkin?'

Mr Flanagan was suddenly propelled from his after-lunch
torpor, back into the world of bureaucracy where decisions had
to be made: he sought for clues among the rows of merchandise
behind the counter and in the shopkeeper's bored face. He hadn't
counted on having to make decisions: he was only looking for
something to pass the time. Any island would do.

'It doesn't matter,' he replied, before he realised that it might
sound odd. But the shopkeeper had already made the decision for
him, reaching for one of the books of tickets beside him.

'Two pounds fifty, please.'

Then, in answer to Mr Flanagan's gaze, he added, 'The trip to
Sherkin is off. Skipper's away today.'

'But — why did you ask me, then?'

'What?'

Mr Flanagan gave up and headed down to the pier, trying to
guess which of the strolling couples and families would be his
fellow passengers. He already regretted his choice of outing,
uneasy at the prospect of the crush on the boat after his period of
solitary contemplation in the rented cottage.

There was no sign of the French girl he had seen in the pub and
later in the only coffee shop: at least, he had assumed she was
French, or maybe southern German, from her brown skin, and the
pannier bolstered bicycle which followed her through the town.
As he watched her progress among the crowds, he had enjoyed

the crab sandwiches in the small dark lounge, comfortably exchanging impersonal trivialities with the barman and drying out from the previous days' weather which had pinned him indoors.

Making his way through the crowd at the edge of the pier, Mr Flanagan felt panic beckon. The boat was small, completely open, with a narrow bench seating perhaps forty, fewer if there was cargo. Around him, at least a hundred people jostled forward to gaze into the murky harbour waters. He held out his ticket to a man fiddling with a rope, determined to get a good seat. As the rope pulled taut, the boatman below shouted 'Careful on the steps, now,' and there was a stampede forward. In a moment, the narrow benches were full and Mr Flanagan was sitting on a coil of rope near the gangway, feeling the gunnel sink further towards the water; still the crowd pushed around him onto the open deck.

With his back to the bows, he was badly positioned to seek out the humped slopes of the inshore islands through which the boat at first inched, hiding as much as possible from the open sea. In any case, the wind and the spray together were destroying his map, so that he had to refold it the wrong way and shove it into his jacket pocket. The boatman began a comic commentary to distract the passengers from their cramped limbs and the low-swaying bows of his vessel.

After a while, as the boat lurched along and the boatman led choruses, an elbow dug into Mr Flanagan's back and was removed.

'I'm so sorry. Would you mind?'

He glanced down and saw a carrier bag drooped halfway across his feet.

'Just for a moment. It's so difficult to manoeuvre.'

The owner of the bag had her head thrust into the body of an Aran sweater. When she was recognisable, Mr Flanagan saw a vaguely remembered face from the beach; or perhaps it was from the little platform suspended over the cliffs at Mizen Head.

'Thank you very much.'

'Not at all.'

The woman was about his own age, apparently unmarried, but not afraid to address him. She looked, Mr Flanagan thought, rather like Mrs O'Brien who organised the whist drive he attended each Tuesday and Thursday: familiar yet formal. Turning back to gaze down the deck at the receding sea, he realised that none of the passengers, except for himself and this woman, appeared to be travelling alone.

'Have you been to the island before?' The woman had not got a local accent; Mr Flanagan tried to identify it as her breath touched his ear, but failed.

'No,' he said, ' — I've never been to this part before. That is, I've passed through ... I usually go on coach tours, you see.'

As he listened to her singsong narration of previous trips to various locations, Mr Flanagan allowed himself to think back to the whist club. The others had not been pleased when he announced his intention to travel alone by car this year: the four of them had always gone together around the country on coach trips, even to Britain once or twice.

'It must be the mid-life crisis.' Over the last trick before the summer break, the others had joked to hide their disapproval, jealous of his dissatisfaction with the annual ritual that cemented their brotherhood for another year of card playing.

'I'm a bit old for that,' Mr Flanagan acknowledged their censure, but stuck to his guns, seeing an isolated week in a rented cottage as an antidote to his ulcerous progress towards retirement. Reading, walking, fishing: these were occupations he could practise at home, as the whist table hastened to point out. He could not explain how the scaffolding of sociability he had slowly built over the years was no longer adequate to stop the gnawing pain in his chest as he lay awake at night.

After two days of storm, there was little of the scaffolding left. Now, he felt more uneasy than ever, seeing too clearly how the children and the couples and the groups of students were laughing at his solitary state. He tried not to think of the series of disasters which had proved his card partners right: the palpitating beam of the lighthouse and the roaring of the wind which had provided an unwelcome *son et lumière* on the night of his arrival; the puncture on the mountain road below the cottage when he stepped out of the car into impenetrable blackness; above all, the death of the rabbit a few yards further on.

Mr Flanagan had been leaning into the steering wheel, peering carefully down a tunnel of mist and rain along the potholes, when he hit the rabbit. For a moment, he thought it had escaped, its tail flipping past the edge of vision as he danced on the pedals and pulled fiercely on the handbrake. The car sagged as he stepped out, then strained against cables and gears on the sloping tarmac.

The animal lay nearby, without apparent sign of injury, only its white tail clearly visible where tarmac met grass. As he stood over the body, glasses fogging in dismay, Mr Flanagan suddenly realised that he was surrounded by absolute emptiness. Somewhere behind him, to his left, the sea thundered against the headland: he had turned inland from the coast a mile back, but the road had twisted bewilderingly since then. Mr Flanagan had the feeling that beyond the glimmering rabbit there was a sharp drop. He had turned and stepped carefully over the potholes and sat again into his car, struggling as he released the handbrake and depressed the accelerator to stop the slide backwards into nothingness.

'Is that the island now?' The woman recalled him to the cramp in his legs, but it was the boatman she addressed. Mr Flanagan craned sideways, almost falling off his coil of tarry rope, and saw that the boat was heading for a steep cliff. When he looked back at the way they had come, there was no sign of a trail on the water and the mainland was out of sight; even the lighthouse which had swept his pillow with unnerving predictability was a scratch on the horizon, far from the powerful searchlight which had transformed his dreams into cinemascapes of barbed wire and machine-guns.

The boat took a long time to dock, manoeuvering between the pleasure yachts and the battered cargo ferries. The woman beside him, purpling in her heavy jumper, twittered and plucked at Mr Flanagan's sleeve to point out the Gaelic names on the pubs, the fishermen's caps, the metal disc of the windmachine just visible on the summit of the cliff. The harbour was too well sheltered from the breeze which whirled the blades above them, and Mr Flanagan felt damp patches spreading under his arms and below the back of his neck.

When the boat finally ground against the quay, he detached himself quickly from the wooden seats and, stumbling up from the uneven cement onto rougher tarmac, found himself leading the woman to the village. With the freedom from physical ache came an urge to command: to his surprise, he discovered himself taking charge, lifting the plastic bag and his jacket over the bollards which marked off the pub's courtyard from the road.

'What about a drink first?'

As they sat among the sleepy Germans and the waiting officials — there was a yacht race in progress, from the mainland to the Cape — the sun streamed down, dowsing the littered tables with outdoor glamour and drying the moisture from Mr Flanagan's back. Busy with arrival, neither the trippers nor the islanders had time to scorn him. He basked, forgetting the desolation of his arrival only forty eight hours ago, realising that he had not thought once of his ulcer or his routine-strangled life since he stepped off the boat onto the island.

'Did I say everyone calls me Margie?' The woman had leaned forward, smiling persistently over her glass of shandy, while he dreamed. Taken by surprise, he revealed his first name to her; she seemed too impressed.

'Such a nice name! I have a brother-in-law called Stephen, such a coincidence ... my late husband's brother.'

As he noted her frank glance at his left hand, Mr Flanagan was first embarrassed, then amused, even elated. The continental weather and the glittering plop of water inches from his feet had induced in him a langour which promoted bravery. He glanced down at his waist and breathed in, wondering if his actual age was noticeable.

'Shall we explore, then, Stephen? The village is just up the road. Oh — I'm sorry, I thought you were finished.'

It had been a long time since Mr Flanagan had heard a woman use his Christian name. He swirled the last mouthful in his glass and drank without haste, wondering what else the island held.

In a few moments, they had discovered the other pivots of the harbour's existence: the farther pub, the general stores and the craft shop which hung half-way up the hill between the pier and the wind machine. Waiting outside the craft shop, Mr Flanagan looked back at the toy harbour and beyond at the first yachts flung in a line on the horizon. He began to review Margie in her absence, then sank again into unreflectiveness. The more active members of the boat party were already disappearing over the brow of the hill under the wind machine, their jackets and jumpers deposited at the pub where the rest chattered or slept among the clutter of wasp-hung glasses. Alone on the slope, Mr Flanagan heard their murmuring along the breeze and smelled the odour of their hot flesh.

Then, as his eyes swept the road again, he saw, strolling past him away from the village, the foreign girl from the mainland. She carried a small, red rucksack which bounced gently across her white teeshirt as she stepped into the grass edging to avoid a lunging car. A tractor followed, blocking his gaze as it inched in a cloud of diesel up the steep incline. When it had passed, the girl had vanished, but Mr Flanagan imagined a glimpse of white at the top of the hill, like the rabbit's tail at the edge of the unknown.

Margie was hovering at the back of the dim shop, fingering emblazoned sweatshirts and peaked sailing caps.

'I won't be very much — .'

'There's no hurry at all — Margie. I won't be back for a few minutes myself. Just in case you needed your bag ....'

He nodded vaguely in the direction of the pub and she smiled discreetly, watching him retreat. Outside, he stepped into the waterfall of light and plunged upward, zigzagging past the toiling parents and children laden down with cameras and bottles of lemonade.

The tarmac wound through the cleft and at first he was conscious only of the towering rocks on either side and the heavy buzzing of insects among the purple flowers at the roadside.

Then, in a few yards he had reached the pass and stood over the descent to the far coast of the island, surprised by the narrowness of the traverse. None of the others had toiled this far, picked off by the steep gradient, one by one. Mr Flanagan panted lightly, his breathing the only human sound he could hear as he gazed down on a second harbour. This one was deserted except for the dive-bombing gulls around the headland, the steep paths converging on the small slipway bare of people, the water empty of boats. As he strolled downward, the blue sea spread at his feet and he wished that he still went in for swimming.

For a moment, he was tempted by the solitude to strip: then he heard a sharp splash. Following the sound with his eyes, he saw after a second or two a head bursting the flaccid surface of the water. The swimmer was making for the rocks half-way around the bay and climbed slowly through the seaweed fringe, her tan showing up against the bright dripping swimsuit. Mr Flanagan thought quite suddenly that he would wave or call a greeting, so well did he feel he knew the girl from tracking her through the town and the steep roads of the island, but then he realised that she had not seen him, or was ignoring any onlookers, face turned towards the water as she dived.

Mr Flanagan leaned against the hedge of fuschia, overcome by the heavy aroma when he rubbed the pink florets between his palms. Time seemed to unpeel itself from his skin, leaving him weightless and soft and without rancour. But, as she dived again, the weather recalled him, unsuspected clouds sweeping up on a chilly breeze to cover the sun and drain the sparkle from the sea. When he glanced back at the pewter water, the ripples of the swimmer's dive were fading and he did not see her head reappear. He waited, staring at the spot where she had vanished and at a wider circle beyond. Then he began to move hesitantly along the wall towards the slipway, considering if he should remove his glasses and his wristwatch, trying not to panic at the heaviness of the water.

'Hello?' he roared, leaning out perilously, then 'Help!' hovering on the edge of the cement as the ends of his laces sucked up moisture. He turned round hopelessly and saw a strolling group on the pass above. Still pinned to the slipway by the leaden seconds, his mouth opened and his arm reached upward.

'Excuse me, please.'

The girl's fingers clung to the edge of the slipway and he almost reached down before he realised he was obstructing her efforts to climb out. She trod water, her black hair slicked back from a cold gaze.

'I'm sorry,' he mumbled as he retreated, pulling his jacket over his head at the sudden downpour which swelled the harbour water and scattered the strollers before him back to the pub.

As Mr Flanagan began the twisting descent into the village, the rain eased and he realised that the afternoon on the island was over. Already, tiny figures crawled towards the boatman to hand in their tickets at the pier's edge. When he got to the boat, he was almost the last to board and he stood in a tiny space in the stern, looking down at Margie. There was nowhere else to sit, so he sank onto the boards at her feet, but managed to turn sideways, pretending not to notice the spare seat beside her marked out by the carrier bag.

'Buy anything interesting?'

'Did you get to see the rest of the island?'

They smiled in embarrassment, until Mr Flanagan looked at the ankle propped up beside his knees.

'Twisted it,' said Margie, 'when I was trying to climb the hill. I thought I saw you head up that way. You seemed to be following....'

As her voice trailed away in a thin whistle, Mr Flanagan felt with rage his face darkening to the shade of the island's wild fuschia.

They both looked landwards, at the short stretch of tarmac leading to the pass below the wind machine. A stiff wind blew the clouds above it in rapid succession and the blue patches were the icy colour of an Alpine sky. Mr Flanagan shivered in his damp jacket, then looked away as he saw the foreign girl running down the road to the harbour.

Watching the breakers snap smartly against the foot of the cliff, Mr Flanagan realised that it would be a rough two hours back to the mainland. If he could sit in the space beside Margie, there would be some shelter in which to study his map; he could point out to her the inshore islands. He cleared his throat, but Margie would not catch his eye, tucking her sweater down around her hips while she peered at the girl paying the boatman. To his dismay, Mr Flanagan saw the girl turn and step carefully among the bodies towards him.

'There's Cliona at last. Always late — she's lucky I kept the seat.' Margie spoke distantly to his ear. 'My daughter came out on the morning boat, to swim in the far harbour.' Taking the carrier bag from the bench, she placed it on Mr Flanagan's left foot. 'I hope you don't mind if I ....' Then she added, as if for an afterthought, ' — but I'm sure you must have seen her there, in the far harbour.'

'No, not at all,' answered Mr Flanagan as the breeze rocked the boat, bowing his head beneath the cliffs and beginning to study his map for the quickest route home.

A DESCRIPTION OF THE
MAIN SIGHTS

Anne stepped out on deck, feeling the muscles of her neck unwind from the rush to the port and the inching drive along the quayside and onto the car level. She recoiled only slightly from the crowds thronging the rails and the children who dashed in and out through them, barely missing her in their headlong flight. Filtered through polaroid sunglasses, their teeshirts and loose jeans seemed the grey garb of displaced refugees rather than the new clothes of tourists bound for sunshine. Although she looked out over the rail at the quayside, she found no clues to the meaning of her slighty surreal vision in the sprawl of the town, above whose monochrome roofs the pale clouds mingled with the light smoke of summer fires. Seeking reassurance, she murmured, 'these people can't all be travelling, surely?'

More eager than ever for the boat to move off, she looked down at the port again. The loudspeaker proclaimed further delays, while the vague throb of the engines beat like an incipient headache. On the quayside below, she could still see a lengthy queue of cars and trucks flanked by uniformed figures. Beyond the barriers, the drab facades of ramshackle houses gave no sign of expectation.

'Are you coming to the bar or not?'

He had followed her as far as the doorway to the deck, but remained with one foot still on the stairs, his sunglasses dark against the pallor of his forehead.

'Steven, it's only three o'clock.'

'All the more reason to get there before everyone else, then.'

Anne turned and followed him into the narrow passages of the ship, the smell and the vibration stirring her stomach. Head lowered, she hurried to stay in his wake, to shelter from the oncoming stream of passengers. A man passed too close and she shrank from contact with his bare arm.

'What's wrong with me? It must be the crowds,' she said to herself.

In the lounge, among the tables and chairs bolted to the greasy carpet, she was suddenly glad to be inactive, occupied only in leafing through the maps and watching the swell beneath the porthole. She took off her sunglasses and blinked at the brightness of the table, a new litany jerking itself through the spools of her memory. Concarneau, Quimper, Dinan: behind each name loomed the ramparts and towers of Brittany's past. Now that she was almost there, the anticipation was stiffening her wrists and making her fingers clench and unclench themselves at random.

Tired of waiting for him to return from the bar, she reached into her bag for the green book and longed for some physical sign of departure: a change in the note of the engines, or at least a lift in the sense of depression which had weighed her down most of the time since they had driven up the ramps and into the clanging hull of the ship. Once they got going, perhaps things would work out the way they always did, like the safe ending of the romantic novel she suddenly wished she had brought.

'Look — the gas rigs. Over there!'

A child's elbow brushed her head. She glanced round and obediently turned to follow the pointing fingers. Unknown to her, the harbour had vanished, the coast was now a low smudge on the skyline and the rigs raised their iron bodies in a last, hieroglyphic signal. That moment, as he returned from the bar, panic gripped her and she rushed to the toilets to retch over a newly scrubbed basin.

'Seasick?' he asked later when she ate only bread, shoving away the lurid collection of salads.

Even after landfall, her body continued to rebel. As they moved eastwards across the flat fields of Brittany, there was endless flatness on each side all the way to the horizon, naked of hedges or hillocks; the villages thrusting up their water-towers at regular intervals were too toy-like to be real. Even the churches which pricked the plains were each emptier and more elaborate, museums disjunct from her expectations. At night, as he dozed over a novel in bed, she struggled less and less avidly with the index of the guidebook.

'Brittany is almost an island'... aptly describes the Breton economy which is marked by its proximity to the sea and its separation from France as a whole.

The landscape, throwing them together, did not encourage conciliation. They argued over small things — which village to visit, whether or not to take the fast and terrifying motorway in place of the meandering local roads. Anne knew the suggested tours by heart and did the driving, but she saw that he was taking complete control of the trip. His stamina grew with each dusty mile they travelled, while her own strength was sucked out of her by the hot, sunless sky which threatened, but never delivered, thunder and lightning. Each morning when they stepped through the door of a different hotel, he would glare up at the unchanging ochre clouds and then at her.

'Most of the people on the boat were going south, you know.'

'Sun worshippers. And we only actually spoke to two of them.'

Peter and Clare had smiled at his jokes over dinner, crossing and recrossing their brown wrists. Anne had watched them in silence, wishing that they too still held hands.

'All the same,' he said more than once, 'they obviously knew what they were talking about.'

As they neared Dinan, the outermost point of their itinerary, she was ready to relinquish the guidebook. On the motorway which ran from west to east across central Brittany, as they passed the signs for the forest of Paimpont, Stephen began to read aloud, maddening her.

During the chilly spring evenings, as the light faded in the garden and the single beech tree grew shadowy, she had yearned to visit the remnants of the great woods, fortification of Brittany in pre-history. She had organised the trip around it, making a list of the towns they would pass and the hotels where they would stay. Now, at the mid-point of the fortnight, her hands seemed stuck to the wheel and she no longer remembered where the list was.

'One star: which means, let's see, "interesting". Too bad — not even "worth a detour". Lucky we're not detouring, then.'

Without the strength now to fight back, she pretended to ignore his tone of triumph, regretting the times she had impressed on him her wish to visit the forest. For an instant, she longed to let go of the wheel, push open the door and roll out onto the cool grass of the verge. The stifling prelude to thunder had continued all week, the pressure growing with each mile they travelled from the sea. Oncoming farm trucks with billowing tarpaulins almost brushed her face through the open windows; she jumped each time she glanced in the rear view mirror and saw it filled unexpectedly with the monstrous fender of a juggernaut.

'Take it easy, darling. We are supposed to be on holiday.'

Catching the stale smell of wine on his breath, she asked, 'You're keeping track of the turns? The sign for the café was almost a kilometre back.'

'Don't worry. I'll make sure we don't miss this particular detour. Pity we don't have someone like Peter and Clare to direct us. But, of course — they must be in "San Trope" by now.'

Distracted in different ways by his mimicry, neither of them saw the turning until it was almost too late. Anne was forced to pull in sharply and reverse, skidding around the wrong side of the corner amid a snarl of horns. They bumped down a rutted track towards a small wood, a blue building flashing past behind the trees.

'There it is, darling, what did I tell you? The best café in Brittany, Peter and Clare said.'

Another steep corner revealed the gaudy canopy. No doubt, thought Anne, as she steered the car under the trees, the water would be grey and the beach littered with dirty plastic bottles; but at least there might be shade from the fierce sun which had at last broken through the haze. Then, as they reached the café, she saw that her anxiety had been unnecessary: although the lake was neither large nor very beautiful, the trees came right down to a sandy beach and there was no one else in sight.

'Steven, look: we have it to ourselves. What about a swim before lunch?'

He hesitated, almost, it seemed, convinced. Then he smiled and waved the green guidebook.

'Bet you didn't know this was the largest lake in north west France? — You go ahead, I'll get your things from the car.'

As he strolled back to the bar, Anne waded out into the surprisingly warm water and watched her pale, distant feet moving on the sand. It was almost too perfect, cloudless above, weedless below. There were no other swimmers and she did not venture out of her depth, wary of sudden rocks and currents. As she stood on tiptoe, with the water lapping her chin, she almost believed that she was at the coast again, poised for the return home. The further side of the lake was hidden by outcrops of forest, among which its blueness vanished; it could have stretched for miles. But she knew that the Atlantic was in reality distant behind her, and that close beyond the far shore was the old frontier of Brittany, leading onwards to remote Normandy farmlands and the central plains of France.

They did not speak much for the rest of the afternoon, lying motionless under the pines opposite the shuttered café, while the clouds banked up on the horizon gradually encroached. Steven slept, but she lay on her back, holding her breath to keep the storm at bay. When the sun eventually disappeared, she could scarcely move from fatigue, watching him wake and clamber to his feet.

'Bloody weather. Good — I see they've opened up the café again.'

In Dinan that evening, they stood at the statue of Bertrand Du Guesclin, soldier and charger blinkered in full battle gear. Standing in the centre of the dusty deserted square, Anne was sorry she had left her sunglasses in the car. Silent except for the crack of the pennants on the ramparts, the ancient town shimmered towards her. Then his self-conscious voice was reading text from the book, and history receded into the same twilight tiredness which was beginning to dust the surrounding buildings with grey.

'Listen to this: one of France's greatest warriors, dubbed knight on the capture of Rennes in 1356.'

He was tremulous with a new interest, straining to move onwards, sapping her last reserves of energy. As they searched for the hotel among the solid buildings of the square, she suddenly relinquished enthusiasm and longed for coolness, even rain, amid the blank windscreens of the cars. Behind her, the warrior was impassive, bored by the heat.

When they sought out their car to unload the bags, there was a scrap of paper tucked under the windscreen wiper: *Hello again! Meet you for dinner at the Hôtel de la Place later?*

'Well, well. Peter and Clare. What happened to the famous trip south, I wonder?'

He sounded almost uninterested, distracted by the potted history he had been reading.

Before dinner, while he roamed the town, she dozed in the dim bedroom, lulled by the steady rhythm of acceleration and sharp braking at a junction below the open window. The green guidebook lay on her lap, but the map of the town was too detailed and the scheme of the main sights, sketched in black and grey, eluded her. She could not even locate the square where they were staying, where Peter and Clare, strangely returned from the far south, had discovered their car; where she had waited for the statue to give her some small sign of recognition. Dozing, she still could not let go of tension, and dreamed of them trapped in the maze of streets, in the network of ramparts, where they would wander separately forever without meeting.

When she awoke, he was coming back into the room, key rattling in the lock. He threw himself on the bed, staring at her.

'You should have come, it was great. You can see the whole countryside from the ramparts.'

She closed her eyes and pretended not to hear, refusing to smile at him.

At half past seven, they went down to the diningroom, but it was empty except for a family group, noisy in one corner.

111

'We're probably too early for Peter and Clare,' she said.

He was not listening, occupied in shuffling through the opening pages of the menu to reach the wine list at the back.

'Does *demi* mean you only get a half bottle?'

'I'm amazed — you read menus quicker and quicker these days. Yes, *demi* means half.'

'Look, we're on holiday, in case you hadn't noticed.'

Anne stared at the linen tablecloth.

'*Monsieur, madame?*' The waiter rapidly filled in the blanks on his order book.

'*Grand, s'il vous plaît.*'

She had toyed with her food while he ate, staring over his shoulder at the door. Now, over coffee in the square, the dusk beat in on her like a relentless inquisitor, circling in the foreign streets among the shuttered houses. She was appalled, mapless.

'Why do you think they didn't come?' she asked, but perhaps she had not spoken aloud: it seemed that he had not heard. She raised her eyes and concentrated on the light fading high above them, between the statue's outstretched hand and the chestnut trees. She was somehow reminded of softer skies to the west, late evening walks in the woods and the fresh smell of birch and spruce after rain.

'How I wish — .'

She jerked back to the square with resentment, surprised nonetheless to hear a note of panic in his voice.

' — I wish that even sometimes we agreed on things. Like this trip, for instance. At first, you were keen to see all the sights, driving here, there and everywhere. Now, when I suggest anything ....'

'I'm tired, Steven. It's too late for this sort of thing.'

'You're right. It is too late.'

She heard his eager breathing and the rasp of his shirt as he turned to her, and recognised an old signal. She listened to him tap out a message on his knee with the rolled up guidebook and her muscles tautened against him, even before he said the words.

'Maybe we could give it a rest for a while — .'

'I think I'm pregnant.'

When he did not say anything for a moment, she spoke quickly, explaining the need to return to the ferry, the importance of early arrangements. As she said 'arrangements', she could feel him flinch, but he said nothing, and his face was turned away when the lamps on the front of the hotel suddenly burst into light. The statue glittered back at them as she reached for the room key.

After they went back up to the room, she quickly packed away everything except her overnight needs. His clothes were still scattered around the chairs; he had climbed into bed and lay facing towards the wall, reading the Michelin. When at last he threw it to the floor and began to breathe differently, she picked it up and packed it too. Then she sat on her bed in the opposite corner of the room, watching the curve of his shoulders rising and falling evenly while she struggled for breath in the stifling air.

Once, when a door slammed, he woke and twisted round towards her.

'Annie, are you there? Why is the light ....?'

She was soothed by his voice when he spoke her name, like the cry of a tired child.

'It's all right, Stevie,' she said, moving over to rub his hair, 'I'm here.'

'Things haven't worked out too well, have they?' he said.

For a moment she felt a stab of fear, but already, now that the bags were packed, her strength was returning. He turned back into the pillow as she suggested they might visit the forest on the way back, and soon, her arms wrapped around his waist, they were drifting off to sleep together on the narrow bed.

The sky leaned on them as they headed away from Dinan, but once they had walked a few yards from the car park, Paimpont was dim and peaceful, silent except for the scrabble of a small bird and their own whispering footsteps. In the centre of the forest, they were alone with the guidebook.

To make sure of keeping Merlin, Viviane enclosed him in a magic circle. It would have been easy for him to escape, but he joyfully accepted his romantic captivity for ever.

She looked away from the dim paths around the clearing as the storm broke at last, watching with relief the heavy drops shattering the pond at her feet. The forest seemed to shake itself all at once, waking from the immobility of the past fortnight as the wind rushed the rain through its dry branches. Suddenly liberated from sickness, savouring the coolness of the moist air on her throat, she looked down at his faint shadow on the humus, and thought of the English Channel once frozen over by green fields, knights in helmets galloping from Cornwall towards this ancient forest of Broceliande; now, only Merlin and Viviane still lingered in the thickets, enthralled.

'Let's put the past behind us,' she murmured when he put his arms around her, silently, the deep blue of his jumper blurring and fading in her vision; it was almost as if he might never speak again.

She did not look back as he steered the car through the wooden gateposts from the forest or as he drove along the straight road amid the hectares of pale green maize and the faint shapes of bypassed villages behind the rain. Her thoughts were focused somewhere deep inside herself on an imminent outpouring, the loss and relief as they reached the ferry port and clattered into the belly of the ship.

Once on board, barricaded from Brittany by the scratched plastic of the lounge windows, she took off her sunglasses and watched him sitting at the bar, sombre in navy wool among the light patterns of summer clothes. All was familiar again, from the tender pain which wrung her body now and again to the accents of the bar staff. Peter and Clare were nowhere in sight, and she waited for Steven to join her, for the trip to be over, and for the bright facades of the quayside to edge past, guiding them onto safe ground again.

CROSSING OVER

Summoned up by the feet of the lunch-time crowds, the dust-filled air of the city danced and wreathed its way along the streets. The breeze was gritty and sulphurous beneath the tongue and the shoppers pinched shut their lips and nostrils against it, against the sweet stench of hot tar and the sourness of unrinsed drains. The sun blazed down from the centre of the once-blue sky through the haze, but no one seemed to welcome it.

To Joe, the crowd waiting at the pedestrian crossing had a ferocious aspect he had not seen before. Around him, prams shoved, shopping bags pushed, trolleys trod on heels. The cars and trucks trundled past chokingly, unstoppably. After a moment or two of standing there, pushed to the very edge of the traffic island, the pent up bodies unnerved him. He prodded Anna's arm, urging her forward even though the signs were amber and the last cars still spurted forward to beat the changing lights.

'Are you trying to get us killed?'

Anna jerked away her elbow and shoved at the lankness of her fringe. Joe saw that this afternoon she was not willing to be amenable. In any case it had been a day to put anyone out of sorts, a morning filled with bad omens. Even as they walked from the flat to the bus stop, a lone magpie had erupted from the belly of a flouncing tree and flicked its white feathers triumphantly. Joe had tried quickly to think of something distracting to say, but had failed.

'Um ... will we go to the pictures tomorrow afternoon?'

'Maybe. Did you see it? One for sorrow.'

Her head bent, she had pulled at her lips with ragged fingers. Joe watched the leaves hanging tiredly from the trees, thinking that she looked older today, the bones of her face more noticeable. He did not believe her or her sister when they told him their ages, a full decade younger than he was. There was something about them, a lack of expectancy, perhaps. During the months that Joe had spent in the spare bedroom of their flat, he had never seen either of them apply for any of the jobs in the small ads. Instead, they helped him to fill out the many similar, though always slightly different forms he posted in the box at the end of the road. Once, Anna had said there was an uncle in Birmingham who would write, and they seemed content to pass the long days in waiting.

'Look,' Joe had said this morning as another long tail dipped and swooped across the road, 'two for joy.'

'No,' said Anna without glancing up, 'they weren't together. It doesn't count.'

Now, as the pedestrian light finally turned green, Joe thought he might grasp Anna's arm once more, this time to steer her down the street to the bus hovering at the stop. He imagined the short trip through the sleepy suburbs back to the dark rooms of the flat, to the strangeness of the mid-afternoon sunlight reflected through the frosted bathroom window.

But as the crowd pushed him forward, it was Anna, not keeping up, who put out a hand to grab the sleeve of his shirt, twisting the nylon in her fingers. As he turned in response to her summons, he heard the bus engine chug, then the tinny purr as it accelerated away without them.

'Have you got a pound or two by any chance?'

Joe reached into his trouser pocket, checking that the crumpled note was still there.

'Sure ... I've a whole fiver.'

'Let's go to the pictures, then. We've more than enough.'

'But it's only Monday.'

'So?'

Joe couldn't think of anything to say in reply, already floundering in the silken net which Anna seemed always to spin around the simplest matters. This time it was about the fact that they always went to the pictures on Tuesday afternoons. As he stood there with the brief pressure of her fingers still echoing on his arm, he realised that this was the only pattern he had been able to impose on Anna's life, convincing her that it was a convenient distance between the Saturday night trip to the pub and the build-up to the next weekend.

'Let's go somewhere out of the city instead,' he said, 'out the Bull Wall — or what about the beach ....'

Anna looked at him sharply, then shrugged.

'God, you're such a creature of habit. If the world was going to end tonight, you'd still want to leave the pictures until Tuesday.'

'No,' said Joe, puzzled at her vehemence, 'I didn't mean it that way at all. It's you I was thinking of — the heat — .'

'All right, all right. I'm only teasing you. Dollymount is cheaper than the pictures, anyhow. Come on.'

As they went down the side streets in search of the bus stop, Joe felt the prickling flood recede from his face, and his jaw unclench itself. Lately, in the middle of an ordinary conversation with Anna or her sister, his words would stumble to a halt and his face become rigid. Whatever he was trying to explain would slip away beneath the girls' gestures of discontent or the rustle of the magazines which they read and re-read.

As the bus swung out at last beneath the railway bridge and along the coast road, the light skipped off the sluggish waves to glitter on the roofs of warehouses and containers across the estuary. Two white sailing boats sat motionless further out in the bay.

'Will we take the yacht out today, Anna?'

Joe made his tone playful, attempting to revive the make-believe and the ironic litanies which had filled the days after they first met. But today Anna did not respond. She stared at the left hand side of the road, where neat garden followed neat garden, the glistening tarmac driveways bordered by glaring white and orange blooms.

'Too calm for sailing today, eh? Perhaps a spot of gin at the ol' club would be more in order ....'

Joe stopped when he felt his words starting to tangle, before the prickle in his skin could begin. He waited while the bus slowed then shuddered into motion again, each time leaving a pair of old men or a woman with toddlers staring after the exhaust fumes. In silence they swept past the top of the palm trees on the promenade, watching the tattered fronds shiver in the hot wind. When they got off the bus and crossed the road at the entrance to the wooden causeway, Joe still did not dare to hold her arm.

Their first steps were quiet on tarmac but then louder over the uneven splintering planks as they left the shore and began to move out above the inlet.

'What's wrong, Anna?'

At first she still did not seem to hear, but then she ran her fingers through her fringe once more and turned to look at him.

'That letter came from my uncle this morning.'

'Oh. Are you going to go?'

Now they were walking along the part above the beach. Their feet shuffled on the cement and sand grains whispered along beside them. The statue was as yet barely discernible, a matchstick at the end of the causeway, but Anna seemed to study it closely. Joe had never liked the way the face was turned away from the land, even though he had been told that the arms were meant to be stretched out to the ships in the bay.

'Of course. We're both going on Friday. There are two jobs.'

They stepped out above the sea, and the breeze sprang from nowhere, carrying to them the odour of the bay and the rotten seaweed that plastered the rocks on either side. Without continuing to the end, they turned their backs on the turgid water and the brown smudge of the southern suburbs beyond. After a moment, Joe found that he could talk without halting of the other people they passed on the causeway, of the dogs, the reckless swimmers and, later, of the bus trip back into the city and out the other side to the flat.

For several nights during the rest of the week, while the girls gathered their belongings, Joe sat cross-legged on the floor and scanned the classifieds, but the small print merely deepened his feeling of being stifled. It was warmer than ever as Friday approached. On the last evening Anna spent hours in a cold bath, and her sister was barefoot as she hopped back and forth across the room, ferrying clothes from one corner to another.

'God, it's so hot. And they say London is like this for weeks at a time ... be a saint, Joe, and open the window, will you?'

Even with the barrier of glass lowered, the traffic was still hushed, scattered by the bank holiday. The bedsit girls who had spent each evening of the past weeks chattering at the garden railings were all gone. Leaning out into the dewy darkness above the chestnut leaves, Joe thought at last of something to say.

'It'll be very crowded, won't it, going tonight?'

'Ummm ...?' Anna's sister was combing out her new hairstyle, her shortened curls removing much of the resemblance between the two sisters. Anna had refused to get hers cut to match, still preferring to spend hours washing and drying the long dark strands.

'The boat, I mean. All the holidaymakers.'

'Oh, well ... yes, I suppose so.'

Anna came out of the bathroom just then, a bathtowel piled high, almost toppling, on her head. Joe thought it was as good a moment as any, and he reached over and pulled the bottle of wine from under the sofa. Anna's sister went to get three glasses from the kitchenette, and Anna took an envelope from her bag.

'Here's our share of the rent for next week — no, go on, take it.'

Joe put the notes in his pocket, feeling a momentary optimism at the feel of the bundle against his hip.

'Will you get someone in, do you think, or will you move somewhere else?'

Joe could only shrug in reply, since he did not yet know what he would do. He had grown used to the flat over the past few weeks, tolerant of its greasy furniture and even fond of the cracked plaster moulding above his bed. Now he tried to remember how he had felt before he met Anna, but all he could think of was the strange sinking taking place in his stomach: he realised suddenly that it was the same panic he had felt when he went to a seance years before. He had known that the woman who ran it must be a sham, yet she had a way of speaking about the spirits of the dead crossing over to talk to their loved ones which had frightened him.

'Maybe I'll go over to see you sometime,' he said suddenly. Anna's sister had opened the wine and as they drank it he told them about the seance, exaggerating the way the table had moved under his trembling hands.

'But why did you go at all, then?' Anna's sister was more relaxed now, her packing complete. Anna still had much to do: he could see that from the way she glanced into the corners of the room and rubbed the towel against her hair from time to time as he spoke.

'It was something to do — I mean, my mother had died ....'

'Go on.'

Anna had finished towelling her hair. She looked at him through the damp strands like she had in the beginning, as if she actually saw him. Then, Joe would have forced his tongue to move, trying to explain why one day, almost a year after his mother's death had sent him to live in the city, he had read the notice the medium put every week in the paper. But today he did not try to explain.

'We forgot to go to the pictures this week,' he said instead.

It was all he could manage, having seen that Anna had already switched her attention elsewhere in the search for something final to say.

'You should come over — give it a try.'

'Yes, I must,' he said.

'We'll be in touch', said Anna's sister.

After the taxi had pulled away from the gate, Joe went back upstairs to the empty rooms and sat beside the window for a while, watching the red streaks of the slow sunset beginning to stretch across the sky. It was very quiet: no sound came from the other flats in the house and the street was empty. When the silence had filled him, he got up and shut the window. Immediately the atmosphere grew close and stale again and he thought of the fresh, salt breezes which had fanned them in their walks along the causeway.

An hour later, when he reached the ferry point, the sea air was colder than he had expected. The weather still held, but the ribbons of cloud in the east had thickened when the sun declined, and now a sharp wind nudged the turned up collar of his jacket. He rested uneasily against the bollards of the harbour road. The trees and the port offices blocked out any view of the pier or the wide bay beyond it into which jutted the wood and concrete finger of the Bull Wall.

The procession to the boat was slowing to a bottleneck; relatives and friends were already drifting back past him to their cars. As the engines began to splutter around him, the last passengers embarked; he had not caught sight of Anna or her sister in the crowd. Then the striped funnel began to move, edging cautiously behind the terminal offices. The wind strengthened, channelled up the narrow roadway, and he hunched his shoulders and walked before it up to the bus.

Among the wrecked seats on the top deck, speeding along the coast and back to the city centre, Joe stared out over the bathing place with its sloping concrete platforms, over the ragged grass to the railway line, over the empty bay to where he knew the Bull Wall, invisible behind the curve of the docks, presented its watchful statue to the beige waves.

For a moment he thought of the coming winter when walking along the causeway would no longer be pleasant. Then, as the darkness thickened and the lights of the city approached, he turned to the tired pages of his newspaper, automatically flicking back past the smudged print of the classifieds to the cinema listings. It was out of habit that he read down the columns: by now it was too late to catch the start of most of the films, and in any case he only went to the pictures on Tuesday afternoons.

CLASS REUNION

The first words, those are the difficult ones: once begun, how-ever ill-equipped, even unwilling, the storyteller may be, the true story will tell itself. Or so went Miss Carson's favourite maxim, certain to be brought out each year on the eve of the creative composition test. 'Be more creative than composed now, girls', floated after us into the desperate silence of English One. I used to think of the gravitational force which, when a flat stone is swung up far enough on its edge, pulls it fully over backwards, willy nilly, to expose the underside; but that was a long time ago, when I was a more assured sort of person. Nowadays, on the edge of my recurring nightmare, as I search despairingly for familiar profiles in the undergrowth, I find myself asking: in what sense of the word is any story true? Then, as the faces finally emerge, as my story begins to coalesce, I wake with tired eyes to a turn of the body beside me, or a murmur from the room next door. The truth recedes behind these things, leaving only a stab of cramp in my calf. I used to be more assured than this, you know, much more assured: it was probably the last class reunion that began to demolish everything.

I think now that I might have worn black, the colour of my nightmare sky. Siobhan was definite in red, a bright, clever red, which clashed in a serious way with the wine gymslip she had been wearing at our last meeting. Mary, elbow bumping mine when she drank, wore a knitted suit: lurexed, batwinged and, underneath it all, the colour of our school uniform.

'What are you having?' I remember I said it a lot, but in fact none of us drank much that night, the better to savour aridly each other's tales. Around us, groups met, merged, dispersed; then left altogether as the barman advanced to buffet the crumbs from empty tables and smear the ash around glass ashtrays with a greying cloth. Under the globular lights, the skins of Siobhan and

Mary were taut and lineless, my own cheek bones ready for flaying.

'You weren't at the last one?' As Siobhan reached for her lighter magisterially, Mary was awkwardly craning around the plastic curve of the seat, trying to see the door.

'The five year one?' I said, then to the barman: 'Three Ballygowans, please. No — as far as I can remember, Sara was going through the measles at the time.'

'How is she?' Mary had been distracted from her watching post, maternal interest overcoming anxiety.

Did I then launch into a mother's manifesto, a catalogue of my foster daughter's virtues? I like to think not. In fact, probably not: the early flashes of tension between us were now building themselves into a ghostly scaffolding as it became more and more obvious that no one else had bothered to come. Our attendance seemed to mark us as social failures, the only ones with nothing better to do — or, as Siobhan put it, over-riding Mary's 'What a pity ...': 'We look like right idiots. I'm meeting Philip at ten, anyway.' She was pleased at her own foresight. 'He's got a lot of casework at the moment.' Mary frowned, looked at her watch and tried to calculate feeds. Instead of being thrown together in adversity, we began bitterly counting the minutes to a decent departure. Even though I had foreseen this as I lurched across town at the rush hour, trapped by my offer of a lift to Mary, some demon in me had leaped to its feet with delight when at last I reached the zebra crossing and the familiar cigarette shop. I thought I caught a glimpse of black veil in the convent garden and for an instant forgot, half hoping to see Joanne at the gate swinging her folder....

It was Mary who began it. Perched on the edge of the seat, she seemed to look into my mind for an appalling instant, before I had time to draw the curtains. I looked away quickly, but she was already speaking.

'So awful, what Joanne did, I mean, what happened to her: does Sara know?'

'Lucky you and Mr O'Neill — I mean, Bill, of course; funny how you always think of them ....'

'Lucky what?' I replied, stung by the sharpness of Siobhan's tone, even if she had saved me from Mary's probing.

'I just meant the way you took on the child, after Joanne — died. I mean, it was very decent of you, considering ....'

It was then that I remembered Siobhan's precise voice, slightly lighter, from Bill's Maths class. 'Mr O'Neill, A must be 25, making Y equal to zero ....' While we had cringed into our copies, longing for the bell, Siobhan had been permanently at attention, frightening him out of his wits, propelling him smartly from the room at the bell's first vibration: this Bill had told me once, as we tried to get Sara back to sleep.

'She never said who it was, did she?' Siobhan winced as Mary kicked her, then carefully bent her gleaming head to study the matching gloss on her red shoes. Now, in the attenuated reunion the three of us were attempting, the only survivors of geography or apathy, any sympathy there might nave been had finally slipped away. The years since I had last seen any of them had edged us one by one into different hierarchies, none of them imaginable as I scratched my name self-consciously below the older etchings on my desk; I had supposed that all of the others had simply stayed hanging about the corner below the crossing, clutching too short gymslips, waiting for my orders. Only Joanne would not be there: that I had accepted, just as, when I looked at Sara, I accepted the flecked brown eyes which matched so well her dark head, had accepted it all from the beginning.

'By the way, are you seeing Bill again? I mean — it was common knowledge that you'd split up, but then we — I — heard otherwise ... hope you don't mind me asking?' Siobhan was brisker and blunter than ever; Mary looked from one to the other of us hopefully and put down her glass on the polished surface, just in time for the barman's passing lunge. I noticed with a strange detachment that the sudden emptiness at her hand scarcely distracted her.

'No. That is: no, I don't mind you raising it and no, I don't see him.'

I still don't know why I told the double lie, unless it was for the confidence I could feel rising as the words slid out without effort, the old skills returning at last; I had always been safe as long as I didn't admit to anything.

'I'm glad.' Mary had muttered it quickly: as I raised my head, I caught the end of a glance between them, like the quick kiss of content lovers. Was it then, I wonder, that I felt the edge of the stone loosen from my fingers, so that I grasped the slime underneath?

'Whispering, they were. They stopped when they saw me.' Mary had raised her voice, pretending to address Siobhan, who marked the pauses with tinkling ice-cubes. 'I remember thinking that funny. Holding hands. Just inside the chapel porch.'

'I heard about that,' I said, very slowly, 'I think you told me at the time.'

'Did I?'

'Well, someone did. It was when her father died, wasn't it?'

'I'm not sure that was the reason.'

'I remember the last time I saw her,' I said quickly, shutting out the babble of voices around me, 'she was all right then, singing to herself. As she passed me, just for a moment, I definitely heard her: "... and the slithy toves did gyre and gimble in the wabe".'

'Oh, come on.'

'That's ridiculous —'

I knew already that I had gone too far, but it had all become too cosy in the curve of the plastic seat, under the soft lounge lights; a drastic change of focus was essential. Better to end it with a joke, better to be accused of a non sequitur.

'There I was, sort of lurking in the cloakroom —'

'Why?' It was Mary, surprisingly, who had dared to ask. Siobhan looked annoyed at her own oversight, then leaned forward expectantly, scenting a kill.

' — getting my coat, of course, imprinting the scene on my mind for future memories, and so on.' I shut off my jokey voice, tried to forget the exultation I had felt that my daily vigil would at last be rewarded. 'It was only after she had passed that I realised it was her — Joanne. Must have been the first time I'd seen her — that anyone had — in weeks.'

' "The slithy toves ..." What did it mean?' Siobhan sounded plaintive echoes of French, German, Latin class. But nowadays her blonder hair was slicked back into an executive bob; and it was Mary and I who gazed at the mysterious papers in her half-open briefcase, hoping for translation.

'Lewis Carroll, or is it Lear?'

'Through the Looking Glass, actually.' Mary, I thought, had not changed: 'Needs to be more assertive ....' I had sneaked a look at all the reports in second year, peering and poking even then, however redundantly: the sparsely scribbled judgements, particularly my own, had always been too predictable. Then Siobhan snuffled and the familiar tune carried me back recklessly from the harsh lighting of the bar to an old pecking order. Even if my learning was suspect, as it often had been, I had always got by on cunning. It was time for the funny voice again.

'Down the corridor she went, sort of chanting it.'

'Mad as a hatter, it was obvious she was going to do it, sooner or later.' Siobhan was unforgiving, her aerated mineral water fizzing through her lips. I smiled to myself at the joke, until I realised, face freezing, that perhaps the tastefully scarlet mouth had after all intended the pun.

'Go on.' Mary was trembling slightly with the excitement of further scandal; I almost succumbed to the mirage of her thirst, yet a new prudence leashed the scene hovering on the edge of my tongue.

'That was it — just that,' I said, and quenched the rising panic of the last day at school. Mine had been the only coat left in the cloakroom as I waited around, hoping for a final glimpse, yet dreading it as I heard the heavy slip-slop, slip-slop of Joanne's sandals on the parquet and waited for her to move into the greenish spot from the corridor skylight. The mutter of the non-sense rhyme seemed quite natural, then: that last time I saw her, Joanne was casting a spell for us all, a bulwark against the terrors of the world beyond the final bell of class ....

I realised that they were still looking at me expectantly. 'What are you having?' I glanced around brightly, but Siobhan was already blinking at a new loungeboy I hadn't noticed.

'The same again, please.'

Mary declined; Siobhan revised the order, naming for herself a drink I didn't recognise. When it became a tall glass, as colour-less as my own, I didn't ask, but received enlightenment nonethe-less.

'It's the new one — they say it's lower in salt content.' Siobhan pressed a tissue delicately to each nostril to conceal her superiority.

Into the tiny pause I dropped a quick question. 'Did you hear about Lucille — three isn't it?'

'I know. So much for Sister Martin and human biology.'

We had switched channels effortlessly; not pax and make up, but rather a suspension of hostilities. Or else, and I fervently wished it so, they had no ammunition left. My guffaws had not been very convincing, but Mary took the cue, picking at the bowl of peanuts with reddening forehead.

'Three's not so many, really.'

'No, quite agreed, Mary. But,' Siobhan paused to sip merrily, 'it's four now.'

'In six years!' I forced my sniggers again. Siobhan was sneezing helplessly at the image of dowdy Lucille involved in the mechanics of it all, but Mary began to protest with surprising vehemence, so that I glanced automatically at her waist-line.

'I don't think we should be — '

'Look, anyone who marries a man like that deserves what they get.' Siobhan was at her most cruel now, yet I egged her on.

'You were at the wedding, weren't you, Siobhan? Best friend, all that?'

'Me? Not at all. Of course, I may have given the impression ... it all happened rather suddenly, if you get my meaning.' We sniggered into our different brands of water, ten years falling away, isolated again in the echoing toilets. Mary hammered at the door, panting from exertion. 'Please. We shouldn't —'

'Oh, for goodness' sake, Mary, grow up. There is the Pill, isn't there?' Siobhan was unctuous, much as she might cross question a dubious client. In her confusion, Mary drank from Siobhan's glass.

'Come on, let's drink to something.' Tired of baiting Mary, wary of further topics, I was impatient to finish off the rituals, even if unable to think of a toast. The evening had been frittered away like another Friday afternoon class. Siobhan glanced at her watch; I could, with annoyance, picture her beau and the exact nightclub to which he would escort her. Mary seemed to have finished the peanuts and, drinkless, stared at the empty saucer.

'To ... the class of seventy seven,' I intoned at last, nervousness making me mumble as we clinked glasses apathetically.

When I left Mary home, she did not invite me in. So, as she scrabbled for her key, I asked, casually, 'By the way, you were the last in the class to see Joanne, weren't you, just before ...?' I was hoping she had been rendered harmless, now that her front door was in sight and Siobhan had retreated. And so it seemed, all steelyness hidden.

'Well, I just saw her on the street. We didn't speak.' She paused then, painstakingly seeking out the unimportant details. 'It was the winter after we left school — she had the baby in a pram, I remember. Just before it happened. Or — in between happenings, I suppose you might say.'

'Did she look any different?'

'How do you mean, different?'

I looked out steadfastly into the shadows, glad that the nearest streetlight was gone.

'You know — different from at school. Like everyone is different.'

'Are we? Well — yes — I suppose I must be different. I wouldn't say Bill is any different, though. You're well out of that.'

Something in her voice invited me to turn my head, pulled it around without my consent, slowly. But Mary was no longer concerned with me, launched on some long prepared lecture. 'You didn't know, did you? But it had been going on for years. No wonder she thought she was Alice ... I can see why she finally crumbled. Tiredness ....'

'It couldn't have been. The nuns would have stopped it.'

I stared out past her head as she spoke on, until her front door rattled open, until she paused. I saw Joanne once again, elegant and amused as ever, lifting the slab over the rabbit hole and sliding out of sight. I felt no resentment that she had left me behind, only misery that my too large body stopped me from following.

126

'Oh, there's Tommy at the door. Must go. Listen — we must keep in touch.'

I nodded and smiled as she bent to get out. Then I drove the car back across the city, slowly, with the radio on, until I came to the coast.

The sky above the sea was blacker than in my dreams, when I stopped where the road met the boulders at the end of the harbour wall. No faces appeared as I gazed out; and when the scattered flares of the lightships began to pulse, no shapes passed in front of them or sought the skirts of the lit-up statue looming on the edge of the wall. Somewhere behind me, Mary and her brood were settling quickly to sleep, Siobhan shunned sleep; it seemed as if I were the only person in the world trying to dream. I remembered Sara and started the engine again, urged my foot to the floor and went home to where the porch light bloomed and Bill opened the door, his hazelled brown eyes welcoming me as the stone fell, back to its place.

So, where is there truth in any of this, or is there a need for truth when I go up to say goodnight to our daughter and touch her mother's hair and watch her blink her dark eyes with sleep? In the end, all I need to do is hold my numb fingers under the tap and run and run the warm water until all the grit is gone, along with another layer of dead cells from my skin.

Custodian of the
Blue Hours

After the rain had stopped, she hurried out into the front garden, ignoring the glances of passers-by as she bent to the flower-bed by the wall. This time, the gladioli had been snapped and torn at random, the two or three overlooked blooms highlighting the damage to the others. She knelt and gathered up the sodden pink and white sprays, hoping to save enough for a bouquet. Then, as she walked to the house, she looked back and saw a trail of bruised petals unwinding itself along the cement path.

In the hall, she watched herself pass the mirror and listened to the silence of the house. The frayed bunches in her hands were already wilting and she decided to take them to the compost heap. For a while then, she sat in her sittingroom, looking at the tarnished silver ranged on the sideboard. Later, as the short day began to peter out, she answered Bruno's summons, and fumbled on her hat and coat.

Along the seafront, they were alone in the space between day and evening: only the empty benches leaped startled out of the dusk. Now and again, the remote sound of cutlery on china penetrated the redbrick walls and drifted down the cropped grass and through the unseasonal palm trees. She knew that it was time for tea, but she did not feel hungry.

They wandered still further on, until they reached the end of the wall, where only a man-made tumble of rocks separated the path from the sea, where she could open her bag and fling the empty vial into the scum at the foot of the stones, craning to watch it tugged outward into the weed. She stepped backwards after a moment, recalled by the rattle of a commuter train crossing the embankment; she turned and began to walk back, the lighted carriages still reflecting bright spots on her retinas, mitigating for a little while the blackness of the path.

By now, even the striped twin chimneys of the power station had vanished, replaced by a ladder of beacons; she could no longer see the estuary tide creeping outwards past the lighthouse to the ocean. All was darkness, deepened even further by the islands of light here and there across the city. When she went up the path to the bungalow, she stepped out of the the streetlamp's halo, so that she had to feel carefully along the contours of the hall door for the metal rim of the keyhole.

After tea, the bell rang twice. Bruno growled at the heavy shape shifting in the porch as she pulled suddenly at the door, jerking the wood against the chain. A man stepped promptly forward from the uneasy shadows of next door's trees, and she clung to the chain until she recognised the reassuring gleam of his dog collar in the light from the hall.

'Good evening, Mrs O'Brien. I'm the new man here ... thought I'd call.'

As he sat on the edge of the sofa and made halting introductions, she sought inspiration in her sideboard. Her ears were alert for the usual appeal for funds as she conjured up the almost forgotten ritual: an evaporated half naggin, a quickly wiped tumbler.

'Please don't go to any trouble ... that's great. Well, cheers, eh ... may I call you Imelda?'

He was one of the younger ones, she saw. As he watched her over the top of his glass, she sat down in the old armchair and gathered her courage.

'It's those boys that are doing it, Father. The ones from the estate.'

'I see. Well, I'll have to have a word then, won't I? Tell me,' he put down his whiskey on the sideboard and pressed together the tips of his fingers, 'how are things since — ?'

She ignored his embarrassed nod at the cards which thronged the mantelpiece.

'It must be stopped, Father.'

'Of course, of course. Don't you worry any more about that. Now, what's this I hear about you and the altar society? Sending out a search party, they tell me ....'

He blustered on for a few more minutes, until he had gulped back the dregs of his drink. After he left, she quickly slid the bolt across, not waiting to see his shadow vanish into the darkness on the drive. Instead, she returned to the sittingroom and leafed through the pages of the old album, startled by the unremembered faces of half a century ago. Harry in scrubbed skin and

double-breasted suit seemed an imposter, the most disturbing of
them all. Only her own debutante portrait was comforting, more
familiar than the twisted stranger who glared at her nowadays
from the mirror. Although she had tried to unpeel it, the perished
mask was fixed immovably to her skull.

It had become harder to venture out, following the old routine:
minimarket, post office, chemist, more difficult to see the
necessity for leaving the confines of the bungalow. Lately, only
her guilt when she saw Bruno scratching at the hall door
prompted her to fetch her groceries and to fill the prescription
which the doctor had given her some months ago — 'to cheer you
up a bit.'

She liked the after effects of the pills, which, instead of resolv-
ing her woolly thoughts, knitted them into a warm grey blanket.
She built up a store against future disappointments, although she
refused to acknowledge that the garden might be ravaged again.
But there were some things the pills could not assuage, like the
pain she felt as she waited in the chemist's each month, and gazed
at the display of perfume, her eyes drawn against her will to her
favourite. *L'Heure Bleue*: it had not been the scent itself she had
cherished each year on her birthday, since she rarely used it, but
the luxury of the same blue and gold box, the comfort of Harry's
dependability.

One day, waiting longer than usual for the prescription to be
made up, her hand hovered towards the display, then halted
when the white coat of the chemist swam into view at her elbow.

'Can I help you?'

'N-no. No, thanks.' She was stuttering, but felt, as she backed
away, that she owed an explanation. 'It's not really my birthday
yet, you see.'

The hum of chatter at the counter was cut off suddenly when
the door thudded behind her, and Bruno's form blurred beyond
her glasses as she bent to untie his lead.

Now that she stayed at home, guarding the flowers from
behind the blinds of the front room, there was no further disturbance. During the weeks of late autumn, she thought that the
young curate must, after all, have taken her seriously. Afterwards,
she realised that the garden, past its summer peak, provided little
temptation; at this season, only a meagre sprinkling of colour
teased the dark green of the shrubs.

As if in warning, the Altar Society sent a delegation. She did
not answer the bell, but through the slats of the blind she could
see them, more stooped than she remembered, walking slowly
away to the gate in black cardigans, heads tilted to view the
ancient scars of her gladioli.

The next morning, she glanced down as she opened the landing window and knew that something was wrong. Then, and even as she stepped out into the sharp air, she could detect no actual change. It was not until, barely breathing, she tiptoed around the lawn towards the rosebed, her remaining treasure, that she saw the damage. The few blooms lay on the soil, their scattered petals like skirts around them, almost as if cast down by a heavy wind; beside them, one last bud had been carefully torn apart.

Feeling nausea rise, she stepped back without touching anything and returned to the house, to turn the keys in both locks, slide the chain across and pull a table against the letterbox. From the front room, she watched the petals shining against the black surface of the bed, until days of autumn wind and rain had tattered and dispersed them.

The level of pills dropped in the last vial, but she could not bring herself to undo the barricades and face the perfume display again. She decided to hoard the few remaining capsules, sleeping when she could in daylight: night was the domain of her custodianship, its commencement signalled by the blue fumes of twilight.

They stayed on guard all night, she and Harry, watching the new moon wax, hard-glazing the garden first with a light rime, then heavier frosts. Although grey shapes moved past sometimes on the pavement, no-one ever crossed the boundary line of the hedge and entered the moon's spotlight, or disturbed the breath condensed on the windows.

It was around this time that she noticed how Harry never slept at all. He remained sitting quietly as she dozed off, and seemed always to be alert, still in exactly the same spot, when she awoke. The only change in him was that he shunned brightness, dodging the sun and electric light in equal discomfort. For some time, they avoided the kitchen at night; then she removed the strong bulb which now irritated her own eyes. All that glare must, she realised, offer unpleasant reminders of the white and sterile hospital room where he had spent the previous spring and summer, where she had brought him peonies, sweet pea and roses, as he shrank down into the sheets, further each day, until only his face was visible.

When she could not reach from the teetering chair to replace the kitchen bulb with a weaker model, she decided that they would live by candlelight, but she stumbled often over Bruno in the dim glow. The dog was restless now that she no longer walked him; on windy days, when the salt breeze carried from the seafront, he raced around the back garden, lunging at her only half in play if she unwittingly entered his territory.

After one stormy morning, she caught some remnant of the dog's energy, some residual need for order filtering through the grey blanket around her head. She had long given up the struggle with the wicked grass which over-ran the cement path and prised up the paving stones of the terrace, and she merely watched during lengthy hours the thin fingers of creeper pasting themselves further across the windows. But the weed, springing up in a hidden corner, could no longer be tolerated, its presence an affront to Harry's husbandry and his regular applications of paraquat to wither the new green shoots into brown sticks, to render the seedbeds sterile.

Now she glared at the plant as it grew handsomely, resenting each sharp-edged leaf unfurling after the rain. On that murky afternoon, she gathered the tools, locked Bruno away and stepped down the path to the miniature cloister between the end wall and the trees. There, her gloves attacked from both sides in a remorseless twisting of the pallid stem, a trowelling of the soil in a continuous circle. The damp loam seemed at first to accept excavation, but, as the leaves burgeoned for the last time, she was betrayed: the white mesh beneath strained and stretched, the plant broke free from its tap root.

For some moments, she knelt over the hole, the limply hanging stem mocking her effort; she thought of the hidden, perennial root system, and her mind leaped despite her efforts to the outline of figures bending to wrench at her flowers. As she slowly dragged herself to the back door, the long grass waved from between the flagstones and the creeper fluttered against the bricks: the garden seemed visibly to be throwing off the last vestiges of respect and restraint.

She made sure then that the back door was locked and walked through the house to the sittingroom, deciding that she and Harry would lose time. It was easy: she left off her watch and omitted to wind the eight day clocks, chuckling as she passed their silent faces, but quietly, so that Bruno would not hear. At intervals, she gathered unread the leaflets and bills which fluttered to the hall floor beneath the barricade, and made a triumphant bonfire in the sink.

She was rummaging in the kitchen cupboards when she found the unmarked bottle of alcohol. If she took a gulp with one of the pills, the effect lasted her for a long time. As the days wore on, she needed to lean into the armchair and tilt the bottle further and further back; Harry was almost his old self then, as they played his favourite game, naming the senders of the black-edged cards which hovered like singed confetti over the mantelpiece. It was a game which made her drowsy: she could doze in the chair for hours, uncertain when Bruno's barking woke her whether it was morning or evening — always the same blue half-light seemed to clog the skyline from the twin chimneys of the power station to the gasometer.

Once, the curate called again, hesitating on the porch, and she roused herself to crouch in the hall with hands clamped around Bruno's muzzle, holding on until she heard the click of the gate. Then she pulled away the table and let Bruno out through the front door. Puzzled with his first outing for weeks, the dog would not at first leave the porch, ignoring her commands as he gazed up into her face and wagged his tail. But, even while she still peered out through the narrowing gap of the door, she saw him shake himself and turn away down the path, the breeze streaming out the plumes of his tail like a banner. As he reached the gate, she shrank back at the figures passing on the footpath, their footsteps hesitant as if they might soon pause.

She fumbled the door shut and turned the keys. Her chest pounded, her hands and feet were icy cold, as she crouched motionless on the hall lino. At last she stirred and stumbled back into the sittingroom. As she moved the knob of the fire, she heard the gas hissing out into silence, no longer camouflaged by murmuring time-pieces or the voices of the past. Then she gazed for a while at the stranger in the sideboard mirror, trying to remember something important.

From the armchair, she trailed her fingers across the floor in search of the bottle, then sucked up the last few drops and discarded the empty vial: it joined the others on the table, among the blue and gold cartons whose bright colours fuzzed.

As the alcohol warmed her, her omission clicked into focus: the billowing gas was unlit. Its fumes scarcely bothered her as she rose on the last pill, curving in a great circle high above the house, beyond the city. The sounds from the front of people calling their dogs, the car doors slamming shut as families returned to their fireplaces, diminished; the haze of dusk entered the room and unsettled the cards on the mantelpiece.

'Look, Harry, look at the cards,' she wanted to say, but was speechless before the peace seeping into her bones. She coughed a little, her breath caught in her throat, and made a small, useless effort to get up. As she dozed off, she was quite secure; just as he used to, Harry would take care of it. She could hear his footsteps in the hall, ever vigilant, ever wakeful: he was arriving now, custodian of her blue hours.

SNOWFIELD

To Isabel it seemed as if winter had arrived without any autumnal warning. In the last week of September the rain began, at first a light sprinkling against the window pane, soon a thickening persistent drizzle. Overnight, the temperature dropped and the cloud descended, blotting out even the fence and the first trees ten yards from the house.

But when Isabel spoke her thoughts aloud, Marie Claire was precise in repudiation.

'No, it will not be winter yet for a while. The snow will not begin until the middle of November — then it will be winter.'

Isabel was watching the diamond rings shine through the dark afternoon kitchen; over and back they glittered as Marie Claire pointed her sharpest knife into the heart of onions and potatoes.

'And how often does it snow?'

As she asked, Isabel was imagining the cycle: the whiteness of the high pastures smoothed by the sun's blade, the last tenuous patches of week-old snow finally scrubbed clean, the naked grass covered again by crisp new flakes overnight.

'All the time, of course, it is always on the ground. Until the spring, naturally.'

Marie Claire had almost completed her tasks. She flicked the shards of potato peel and the delicately curved brown onion skins into the bin; she had not winced as the pungent vapour spurted from the parting layers of filmy flesh. She shrugged, walking away across the kitchen, anxious to get on with something else.

'The roads are kept clear, of course. We use chains. Except for Madame Simon — she has to come across the fields from her farm. You should ask her about the winter — she is here all the time, after all.'

'Oh.'

Despite Marie Claire's obvious annoyance, Isabel was driven to a further question.

'So how long will we be staying here?'

'We? Until Stefan has done enough work on his botany thesis. Probably we will go when the snow comes. — Now, it is time for the next feed, I think?'

Isabel was dismissed. As she plodded upstairs clutching the still unaccustomed paraphernalia of babycare, she remembered her mother's reaction when she had announced her plans for the year after school.

'It doesn't sound very exciting, does it?' she had said, bowing her head to her embroidery in disapproval.

Lately it seemed that her mother was right: since the departure of Stefan's parents for the city, the three of them remaining had rarely met, each following a specific routine in a different part of the house — Isabel generally in the nursery, Stefan always in the study directly beneath, Marie Claire in her bedroom presumably engaged in the tasks of household management.

Now Isabel sat on in the dull light of another autumn evening, waiting for the dinner bell to release her from solitude. When at last its sound rose into the still nursery, she was taken by surprise at how quickly the room had grown dark. The baby seemed unconcerned; his regular sucking merely relaxed, his mouth slipping from the teat of the empty bottle. She got up and laid him down on the changing mat; then she went to the window, reached out and drew the curtains between the shaded room and the shadowy valley.

It seemed so long ago now, that churning excitement of plummeting into France, timetables meshing to carry her through the Paris of her dreams, then away to this evening and this room. The taxi-ride through stately boulevards and across wide, white bridges until she reached the au pair agency, the night train to the south, the country bus and that final car trip across the mountains: all had mysteriously slotted into place, as if destiny awaited her at this particular point in time and space, this especial valley far and high above the mundane world into which she had been born.

When she first arrived, the mountains were more than she had imagined. She had stepped out of the car and tried to absorb all at once the late summer dazzle of the pastures, scarcely noticing the array of people grouped beneath the porch until Marie Claire began the introductions.

'Maman, Papa — this is Isabel. Isabel — my husband, Stefan.'

Then she had forced herself to be polite, saving up for later the details of the chalet rising beyond them. Long afterwards, when other memories of that time had faded into oblivion, she could remember the facade clearly, the carved oak balcony and half-shuttered windows floating behind shafts of early morning sunlight; and she thought of it always as she had first come upon it, forgetting other views from the side or above, in rain or behind mist.

They had all shaken hands then, while somewhere a dog barked, the sound lifting from far along the valley's steep side. The older man and woman were obviously Stefan's parents, both from their physical likeness and from the close knot they made, a little apart from Isabel and Marie Claire. Then the older woman hung back for a moment and spoke to Isabel in a manner which was almost too casual; Isabel sensed that her successful assimilation into the household was at stake.

'You are not afraid of dogs, I hope?'

The woman's tone was neutral, but her mispronunciation of Isabel's language almost deliberate, as if to underline her dominance.

'No, not at all,' Isabel heard herself replying, 'we have dogs at home.'

The other nodded, her expression unreadable, but somehow Isabel thought she had crossed an invisible line between servanthood and a tentatively bestowed equality. As if to confirm this, the woman said as they entered the hallway, 'By the way, I am Yvonne, and my husband is Gilbert. This is less formal, I think.'

That first morning, as they sat around a dark wooden table eating brittle toast and drinking coffee from cups shaped like soup bowls, Isabel still felt unreal, as though she were taking part in a play for which she had not rehearsed enough. Stefan and his father conversed in an undertone at the far corner of the table; opposite them Yvonne conferred permission for their discussion by her silence and precise gestures among the cutlery and the food; Marie Claire dropped occasional, disregarded remarks into the murmur.

Isabel pretended to eat, but consumed very little, occupied as she was with further study of the household. She noticed how Marie Claire persisted in addressing herself to the entire group, although it was obvious that only Isabel was moved by politeness to give any response, and how the upright, unshakeable set of Gilbert's shoulders was echoed in the tiny swagger with which Stefan's every gesture was imbued; she even saw how, after a certain amount of time had elapsed, Yvonne began to glance at her watch until the men looked up, saw her, and began to finish the rest of their food.

'Marie Claire, do I hear the baby?'

Stefan had paused then, eyes raised to the ceiling, blond strands falling back from his forehead. Everyone immediately stopped eating, and to dull the newly minted silence came the high-pitched mewling which had been teasing the corners of Isabel's mind for some seconds.

At the end of that first long day of routine, she had stood at the clothes-line outside the kitchen door. Fastening her cardigan under the cool evening shadow of the house, she watched the miniature garments bobbing on the taut wire against the arch of darkening sky, and sensed the seasons to come. In the late August chill was contained the threat and promise of monochrome months, the endless greyness of mist and rain, and then the whiteness when the wind would blow silently over the levelled valley.

In the early days of October, after the steady rain had washed the light from all their faces, Stefan and Marie Claire went away together to Italy, to see the museums. Their holiday seemed unplanned, Marie Claire's sudden flurry of preparation uncharacteristic.

Isabel felt quite calm as she watched them get into the car, relieved that they were going away and that she would be granted a small respite from the struggle to obey their silent instructions.

'We shall certainly phone tonight from Milan,' Stefan said as he stowed their cases in the boot. Solemnly then he shook her hand as though they were strangers; which they almost were since he did not concern himself with the domestic needs of his child. Then Marie Claire started the engine with a grinding roar.

As the car spurted away through the gates, Isabel stood in the centre of the driveway, waving, and shading her eyes with her free arm. Her eyelids stung against the brightness of the rising sun on the peaks, but she waited until the last reverberations of the engine had died away from the cool air of the valley. Then she turned and walked slowly back to the house, placing her feet with exaggerated care into the centre of the deep ruts in the moist clay.

Yesterday there had been unbroken mist and rain, but today as she stepped into the dark hallway shafts of newly washed sunlight struck the floor purposefully before her, turning the wood into a shining platform for her steps. On this blue and gold morning, autumn seemed to have been routed for a little while by the last breath of summer; as Isabel moved through the warm islands of light in the kitchen, she caught a glimpse of two birds preening themselves outside in the soft grass of the lawn. She did not know what kind they were, but they seemed somehow settled there, preparing to over-winter in the high valleys.

All that day, as Isabel tiptoed across the wide, bright nursery, she felt light-headed, her stomach taut, torn between the anxiety of absolute responsibility and the elation of freedom from the prescribed routine. On this particular morning she could walk the baby unselfconsciously across the creaking floor, unimpeded by what she always imagined were the motionless listeners below. Perhaps she simply could not hear their conversation through the thick wooden floorboards, or perhaps they had already gone to resume their tasks; but she always felt that instead they were still sitting there at the large oak table, their eating or reading broken off abruptly, heads tilted upward to catch the signals of her progress. In her image of them, Stefan's hair flapped back from his forehead as it had that first morning and his gold watch glinted against the pale hairs of his wrist, while Marie Claire kept her head averted and tapped her fingers in time to Isabel's tread.

Still walking, Isabel raised her eyes to the mountains. Unconstrained by the family's custodial presence, it was the first clear view she had had, and only now did she notice the particular details of the higher, permanent snowfield. What had seemed a uniform expanse of white was in reality scarred by innumerable features — the darker folds and creases of rock protruding through thin ice, the blue-glazed, frozen force of a glacier's path, the iconography of tiny tracks and prints which could have been merely a game played by the wind, or the track of chamois.

'Wasn't it a lovely day?' she said later to the housekeeper who had come to prepare supper. But Madame Simon merely turned her head slightly and smiled. Then Isabel remembered that out of habit she had spoken in English.

'The weather was very fine today,' she began again, and this time Madame Simon nodded comprehendingly as she sliced through milky potatoes and ranged them neatly in a casserole. Then she said, 'but of course this will mean a hard winter.'

'Really, why is that?'

Isabel was fascinated by the certainty with which Madame Simon spoke.

'You see, the same air which brought sunshine today to the valley will also bring the snow in a couple of weeks. It will be early, although perhaps by not more than a day, but it will be very heavy. And, of course, all the birds have left early.'

'But I saw a pair on the lawn this morning.'

Isabel felt somehow shocked that Madame Simon should be wrong.

'Yes — and I saw them too, after lunch. But they were preparing to go, cleaning themselves. And I did not see them this evening.'

After a while, when they had moved back into the kitchen and were drinking hot chocolate to send Madame Simon on her way, Isabel felt that she was being studied. She turned her head and saw the housekeeper smiling in an odd way, almost concernedly.

'How do you find Monsieur and Madame? They have been spending the summer here for a few years now.'

'Oh, they're fine. They seemed a bit ... rushed, I suppose that's the word. Yes, rushed. When they set off for Italy.'

'Yes.' Madame Simon shook off a frown with a further question.

'And how do you like our valley, Isabel?'

'It's wonderful. I'd love to stay here during the snow.'

Isabel had surprised herself by bursting out with her feelings in a French which she had not formulated in advance.

'Yes. The snow is wonderful, but also very strange, when we are alone here, closed in, high up on the mountainside. Things can happen, you know.'

'Things?'

But then a car horn sounded outside and Isabel was taken to greet Monsieur Simon, who expressed a fatherly concern that she was to be alone in the house. As she waved them off from the front, the porch light showed Madame Simon turning and peering back until the darkness enveloped her.

After supper, Isabel pulled the curtain aside and saw that the stars had been blotted out; once again, the valley slumbered in thick mist. She returned to the sofa and stretched out in front of the log fire. Directly above her, the baby slept; beside the great central chimney Isabel dozed, dreaming of snow, of the next few weeks when the landscape would be levelled and transformed, the snowfield of the mountain peaks merging into the valley. Perhaps then, she mused, she could somehow cheat time and habit and catch once again the magic of her first sight of the peaks, when all her chocolate-box pictures came to life, outside history and beyond the world of drudgery.

Some time later she woke abruptly. The telephone was throbbing in the hall, with a pulse which was strangely threatening, so that she did not really want to go and answer it.

When she returned to the room, she was fully awake. The dim glow in the fireplace told her it was very late, yet Marie Claire had not remarked on it, seeking only the minimum of conversation to establish that she and the baby were all right. She could scarcely decipher Marie Claire's words against the background noise of talk and laughter, movement and doors; and Marie Claire did not seem to be able to hear when Isabel asked her about her holiday or what the weather was like. Isabel's thoughts were confused as she sat again before the grate, slightly nauseous from her dreams, yet reluctant to climb the stairs to bed. She watched tiny avalanches of ash break the silence with their fall.

At the end of October, Marie Claire returned alone and untanned, and the weather began to change once more. There was a gathering heaviness in the chill air of the hallway and stairwell, and Isabel felt herself weighed down as she moved about the chalet. It could have been the change of season, the fact that her routine was now forced back to its old patterns, or the questions about Stefan which she did not have an opportunity to ask. Marie Claire did not speak much, and stayed mainly in her room, but when she did emerge, orders were given and instructions issued, until Isabel's head reeled and she longed for a fresher climate.

Then, one night, as she opened the hall door and leaned out into the searing cold, Isabel knew that it would soon snow. There was complete darkness in the valley, and no sound: the canopy of cloud had thickened and swelled as though it were gathering enough flakes to bury the world. But above all there was the smell: beneath and beyond the sweet cover of woodsmoke from the chimneys above her head, a cold metallic whiff, a hint of incense.

Into the air rose the sound of a car approaching, then halting. A moment later, Isabel saw Stefan carrying his case with difficulty along the uneven driveway. Before he could see her, she moved inside; for a moment she thought of telling Marie Claire, but instead she hurried upstairs to see to the baby.

Before dinner, Isabel went over to the chest of drawers and took out the velvet bow she had been saving for a special occasion. As she pinned it carefully at the crown of her head, she saw her reflection shining in the old mirror, and for the first time in weeks she felt as if everything was turning out right, as if the shattered fragments of her destiny were at last being pieced together again.

'Soon it will snow,' said Stefan as he took a second helping of grated carrot from the dish.

'Yes,' said Isabel, 'I think so.'

'Soon it will snow,' Isabel repeated softly to herself, and listened sharply for a moment as though she expected to hear the flakes falling. But just then, her fork half-way from her mouth, she felt the chill of Marie Claire's gaze and turned to meet it, wondering if her whisper had been misconstrued. But Marie Claire was looking not at her but straight past, at Stefan. Before she spoke, she raised her napkin and dabbed at an invisible particle of food.

'Yes,' she said, her voice impassively continuing the conversation while her eyes burned with a feeling Isabel could not identify, 'possibly tomorrow night it will snow.'

'What about tonight?'

Isabel was taken aback at her own temerity; a moment ago her usual embarrassment would have held her back from such a contradiction, but now she felt they were too tightly bound together, the three of them, by Marie Claire's gaze.

It was Stefan who replied, looking at her with his crystalline smile, 'Not tonight. It's too cold.'

'So,' said Marie Claire, now also looking at Isabel, 'we will leave tomorrow.'

'Yes,' said Stefane, 'I'm sure you'll be glad to see Paris at last.'

'Of course,' said Isabel, 'that will be very nice.'

As she thought numbly that they had never before held such a long conversation, Marie Claire and Stefan rose from the table and walked together past the fireplace to the door. Isabel suddenly saw what she had not noticed before, the fact that no fire had been lit that evening, although the sticks and larger pieces of wood had been arranged in the clean grate as usual. She also realised that she must have misheard Madame Simon's final *'adieu'* as her more usual *'à demain'*.

When the door shut behind them, Isabel sat on, watching the butter glazing congeal in the dishes. After a while, she rose and cleared the table. Then on an impulse she reached for her coat and stepped out through the kitchen door.

With nightfall, a thin mist had risen from the lake, so that the valley and the wall of rock beyond were sunk in obscurity. There were glimmers of light around the terrace from a vapid moon, and she could enumerate with trailing fingertips the damp rail, the plastic chairs and the low metal table. After a moment she dared look up, but the belt of sky directly above the roof was partly veiled by wisps of vapour, and no familiar planets or star configurations were traceable in the studded velvet.

'Looking for shooting stars? November is the right month.' Stefan's head gleamed briefly as he stepped forward from the inky wall of the house.

'Want to have a look?' he said, bowing his head momentarily and handing her the glasses which hung around his neck. As she tried to line up the eyepieces correctly he remained standing behind her.

'You should refocus them if necessary,' he said. But no matter which way she turned the small knob all she could see was a blur of light and dark, as though the stars were whirling past them.

'I'm afraid I'm not very good at this sort of thing.'

'Here, let me show you.'

He moved towards her but she was handing the binoculars back, unwinding the cord from her fingers.

'Thanks,' she said again, and he seemed to shrug as she walked away into the house.

The next morning a new kind of emptiness enfolded the chalet. Isabel had woken to a pervasive quietness instead of the bustle which she had expected; even the baby's cries were muffled by the white canopy which during the night had been flung over the eaves of the house. When she opened the balcony window to touch the whiteness, some of its compactness unfolded and fell inward about her feet, melting quickly into dull streaks on the polished floor.

Before breakfast, as she fed the baby, Isabel heard the hushed voice of Marie Claire on the telephone. At the table, both she and Stefan were tight-lipped.

'We shall go as soon as the roads are sufficiently cleared,' she said in reply to Isabel's question, 'since the snowfall was so heavy last night. Tomorrow, probably.'

Stefan rose abruptly from the table, leaving Isabel and Marie Claire to finish their meal in silence.

Altogether it was a strange day. As she moved about the house Isabel glanced frequently out at the single glistening snowfield beneath a sky still weighty with cloud. She thought of Madame Simon's warning: 'Things happen.'

Whether because Marie Claire had not thought to phone her, or because the farm was snowed-in, Madame Simon did not appear. Instead, Stefan cooked the meals; Isabel came upon him in the kitchen frequently, although he seemed not to notice her. Once, Marie Claire was with him; she stood chopping at the counter and spoke to Stefan in fast French which Isabel, sterilising the set of feeding bottles, could not follow. However, there was no need to understand the words; their sharpness threw icy darts into her heart and she waited in clenched embarrassment for the water to boil under the saucepan of bottles and teats. When, after an interval that seemed endless, she had finished her task and could leave, the nursery was a welcome refuge.

In the afternoon she piled on her heaviest jumpers and stepped out onto the balcony. The cold air seized her throat, making her cough: the effect was exhausting rather than exhilarating.

She stood for what seemed a long time. No-one had yet thought to shovel the tiles clear and when she stamped her boots she created a small circle of impacted snow. A great wave of sadness was engulfing her. She listened to the stillness of the snowfield and the silence of the great peaks: all was too perfect, too unchanging, reminding her that tomorrow when she was gone this scene would remain, even the small track she had made on the terrace smoothed over, cleared of any impression.

'Such a heroic girl, Gerda, wouldn't you agree?'

'Gerda?' she said, sidestepping Stefan as he moved to the rail beside her. She felt his breath brush her ear, and wondered how long he had been watching her.

'You know the Andersen story, I presume? The Snow Queen?'

'Gerda was the girl who rescued the boy from the snow queen, wasn't she?'

'Very clever, Isabel. Yes, her tears melted the sliver of ice in his heart.'

Desperately she tried to concentrate on the snowfield, to preserve her vision of the place, but Stefan's arm was suddenly around her, pinioning her thoughts. Like the stars she had tried to focus on, the picture she held of her life blurred, as though she was swept at unimaginable speed along the seasons. She watched in horror as the second was caught up and swallowed by the minute, the minute by the week, until she stood in the midst of great spinning shadows which her flailing arms failed to embrace. Then she awoke, turned away abruptly and said, 'Excuse me, I think I hear the baby.'

By the next evening they were in the city as planned, and the white-mantled valley might never have existed. The snow melted rapidly as they descended into the foothills, sliding away beneath the car's tyres at the edge of the motorway. When they arrived, Paris was noisy, more commonplace than she could have imagined, utterly transformed from the mirage of space and light she had traversed months earlier. She had not remembered the many lanes of cars gunning their engines as though orchestrated, nor the screaming jets which, one after another, grazed the roofs of the suburbs like bullets missing their target.

The first night in the city was laden with fog. Isabel stood by the window of the apartment and saw that the stars were barely visible above the fumes. She waited until her feet became chill, but the heavens remained distant, the constellations receding as if she had again put the wrong end of a telescope to her eye; it seemed that there were no shooting stars in the city either. They were firmly back amid the greys of autumn again.

'Sleep well?'

The next morning Marie Claire was pale and calm, utterly normal, no trace remaining of the emotions which had convulsed her as they left the valley and Stefan behind. At one point, when she stopped the car and laid her head down on the steering wheel, Isabel had to lean forward from the back seat and pull sharply on the handbrake: it had been at the steepest point of the road, the top of the long slope out over the head of the gorge.

'Are you all right?' she had asked, but Marie Claire had merely sat straight again, let off the brake and driven on. Isabel watched

143

the back of her head during the long trip and thought of the night they had all spent wakefully, Isabel lying rigid in her bed, listening to the raised voices which came up through the floor. At last Marie Claire had come to rouse her and she had taken the swaddled baby across the yard to the car in the muffled dawn. She had stared at the condensation trails on the windscreen for hours, it seemed, until Marie Claire came running from the porch with her bags, grim and silent as she bent to turn the keys in the ignition. Behind them the chalet squatted bemused and as always half-shuttered, as if not yet aware of its abandonment. It might indeed have been empty; there was no smoke from the chimney and no movement at the windows as they departed.

'Are you sure you are not weary?' Marie Claire was asking again in the chrome Paris kitchen. Isabel could only bow her head, but Marie Claire was not waiting for an answer. Instead she was saying in a bright, swift voice, 'He had a woman in Italy you know, that was why he brought me there. To show us to one another, I think it was.'

Marie Claire dipped her head and drank from her bowl of coffee, then pushed her plate of cereal away across the shiny table.

'I must go to see my solicitor,' she said calmly, 'about the money and the baby. He shall not have anything.' She paused for a moment, then added, '*L'Italienne* will not take him on, you understand, without the money.'

'I-I'm very sorry about it all.'

'Don't be silly,' said Marie Claire briskly as she stood up from the table, 'it had nothing to do with you.' Then she turned and smiled, almost sweetly, to where Isabel sat amid the remains of the breakfast. 'He made passes at all the au pairs, you know.'

When Marie Claire had driven off about her business into the city traffic, Isabel realised to her surprise that she was almost content. The long ago impulse which had brought her here had been completely eroded by the past weeks, and she could even now barely remember much of the three short seasons she had spent in the valley — a vague image of Stefan's mother, the dazzle of sunlight on the windows of the chalet, the dogs barking in the pastures lower down. Yet this did not perturb her. Somehow she still believed that everything must return to the way it had been, the three of them locked into the valley by the snowfield and the vast silence.

In the years afterwards, Isabel wondered at her own naïvety. This strange state persisted even when she saw Marie Claire tearing up the letters with the valley postmark which arrived each morning and afternoon; or when, at the same hour each night, she heard the phone being answered and slammed down again almost immediately. Even the night that Yvonne called and later came in to look at her grandson slumbering, leaning possessively over the blond curls which flopped like his father's onto his forehead, Isabel still hoped that she would one day again stand in front of the sunlit wooden porch surrounded by the same group as before. When Marie Claire muttered as the lift bore her mother-in-law away, 'She need not think he will see much of the child,' it was Isabel who consoled her, not believing that the struggle would ever have to take place.

But after only a week of the new routine, just when she had begun to think of venturing out into the city, Isabel found herself being driven by Marie Claire to the airport. The baby had been left at a creche on the way, but no proper explanation was offered until they were waiting in the departures lounge, coffee glistening tepidly in thick white cups on the table.

'You see, I must get a job,' Marie Claire said carefully. She sipped her coffee economically. 'Otherwise, I will not be able to support myself or the baby. And then, he would try to take the child.'

'But, when are you going to see Stefan?' asked Isabel, still nursing a gleam of hope. She looked at Marie Claire's long nails and careful make-up, which even now did not crack.

'Stefan? Never. I will never see him again.' Then she put down her cup and glanced at her watch. 'Unless, of course,' she added briskly, 'in the court.'

Isabel bent obediently to gather her hand luggage, leaving her coffee to form a stagnant ring in its cup.

As the plane banked, and the cloud rushed in to fill her vision, Isabel realised how completely the passage of the past three seasons had quenched her dreams. She felt no curiosity now about whether Stefan or Marie Claire would settle the divorce amicably or otherwise. Nor did she feel any sense of contributory guilt; there was no self blame that she should somehow have prevented the breakup of the marriage. This numbness had nothing to do with the incident on the terrace, nor the suddenness with which she had been sent home. She had merely realised that destiny was something which only happened to other people: she would always remain a spectator. In the long silences of the chalet, Isabel had begun her apprenticeship, foreseeing it all as she watched the features of Stefan and Marie Claire merge in uneasy truce in the face of their child. Things had happened, and now she could merely return home to take up the threads of existence in a land where snow turned grey and melted before it had a chance to form patterns on the ground.

INHERITANCE

At dawn, Louise jerked upright from the pillow, then sank back again, remembering. All through the darkness of night, the shelter belt of elms had rustled. Rigid in the narrow coverings, she had desperately sought sleep, but remained blind and open-eyed, listening to the rain whistle down the sloped roof. At last she had dozed, swinging out through the elms' branches, until she found herself pushed firmly back to the attic by the frantic morning traffic of the crows.

She was alone in the attic, as she had been alone for the past five days. Richard and Anne had not yet arrived to fill the void of her caring; instead there was only the greasy soil of yesterday's grave underneath her fingernails. She had been embarrassed about the melodramatic gesture, unsure whether her tidy mother would have approved, forced to it as the leading mourner by the expectant pause from her aunts and uncles. Afterwards, when they returned to the house, a single wisp of duck down had floated on the pond, tantalising her memory, but she had lost it from sight beneath the rush of polite arrivals.

Now she stepped reluctantly out of bed to the faint smell of hot toast and the scraping of a knife on crusts. From the vantage point of the attic, the sounds of farm life were muted and almost unrecognisable, but, as though the television had been switched on halfway through an involved drama, her childhood discomforts were conjured up anew from the vague bustle below.

'And how many eggs will you have this morning, my dear?'

Fastidious at eight years old, Louise always wanted to cringe away from the way her aunt tickled her chin, lifting it with a rough forefinger. 'Just one, please.'

Aunt Mary leaped away to the range and the sausages all gave a little hop in the air as she shook the pan. Their spicy smell rushed in a hot wave across to her as she tasted a large glass of orange juice. She wrinkled up her mouth — it was too sweet, undiluted — and pushed the glass out of *sight while she poured milk on her cornflakes with the other hand. A soft slop of milk and cereal overflowed onto the wooden table: guiltily, she smeared it into a less obvious stain before anyone could notice. She felt too full before she had eaten half of a sausage, but the anxious gaze from the other side of the table made her continue to push the rest of the fry around for a minute before she gave up the struggle.*

Dowsing her face and neck with warm water, Louise braced herself for the day, conscious of the faint sounds below as her aunt interrupted the routine to make a late breakfast. Almost before the last step of the stairs had creaked her arrival, she was ushered to the table; afterwards, the delph was cleared away quickly before she could rise or voice an offer to help. Aunt Mary kept her head half averted, speechless without the interpretations which had been provided by the mother and older sister for all their previous encounters.

Aunt and niece, they had never seemed less akin, except when the rift first occurred, sometime around a twelfth or thirteenth birthday. Louise could not remember the precise year, but the interpolated conversations were only too fresh in memory. 'Two spoons, is it, Louie takes?' had made resentment flicker for the first time as, the claims of her pubescence unheeded, she slouched forward and silently took the offered teacup from her preoccupied aunt's hand. Nothing, it seemed, had changed: yesterday, she had heard Mary say of her, 'Anne's child,' answering graciously for her the questioning looks which accompanied the formal words of condolence from faces she did not remember.

When she was very young, her first glimpse of new whitewash and gleaming churns had sat, oddly, with her father's talk about the 'old place'; now, glancing around at the greying walls and the cobwebs over the sink, Louise saw that the house had been steadily sinking beneath the weight of all the years of her absence: the years when Irish college or school trips abroad had been escape routes from the perpetual childhood imposed by the farm. More than the surface decrepitude, that teenage betrayal had transformed the house into foreign territory.

She stood up and stretched as Mary left the kitchen with a pail of leftovers for the hens. Moving over to the narrow window, she stared past the gaggle of magpies rising from the orchard and out beyond the henhouses and the sheds. She no longer needed to stand on tiptoe to see through the dusty panes, but still she blinked at her first view of the land: African veldt or Russian steppes could not have been more unfamiliar than the endless slope of the field up to the faint shapes of hedge and ditch on the horizon. It was a boundary she had never dared to investigate, since even the farmyard offered tests she could not pass.

'Come along, Louie, and I'll show you the late calf.' Her uncle had smiled as she eagerly grasped his hand, imagining from this strange phrase an animal small and vulnerable, exhausted from the struggle to catch up; another being at a loss in the brutal world of the sheds and the byre.

So, she was carefree as she kicked her boots through the muddy pool of the doorway, but when she got inside, the lumbering bulk of the bull calf in the cramped stall shocked her. Worst of all, there was a witness to her discomfort: Teddy, neglecting the jobs that usually kept him limping around the farmyard. As he fondled the calf's neck, she pressed against the wall of the shed in terror at the splaying legs and the wet, red mouth, disbelieving his tale of the coddling they gave the fierce thing after its birth a month ago. Teddy moved through the soggy straw with a bucket and she stiffened as the calf stampeded his hands and sucked frantically at his fingers, waiting for the sound of crunching bones and Teddy's screams. She jumped when something brushed her head: but it was only her uncle's hairy jacket swinging as he bent forward.

'Wouldn't you like to pet him? Give me that, man, we'll let the child have a go at feeding him this time.'

Teddy grinned as he turned. 'Surely, surely.' He egged her on. 'Let's see the girleen do it.'

Louise remembered only one thing clearly: their howls of laughter following her flight to the house. It had been that incident, she considered now, which had set the seal on her rebellion against the place. All that day, she had railed at what seemed to her the pretend forgetfulness of her uncle; things got even worse when he came to collect the three of them for the legendary trip to the county hospital, which her father never forgot to recount on the most embarrassing occasions, like the first time she brought Richard home. Afterwards, as she walked him to the bus, Richard had merely smiled at her without speaking, which was somehow worst of all.

In the car, listening to the talk of her parents and her uncle, she had watched the bunched trees around the farmhouse vanish in the rear window: like the thin-limbed old men she had seen in the churchyard after the funeral, they stood silent and gaunt, waiting for a gust of wind to bend them towards each other, whispering. Now, as then, she longed for her home in the city, a small house tucked away with a crowd of others beside the river. The misty cranes and warehouses were as tall as the trees here, but loomed in a friendly way, as if to answer the soft plucking of the river against the stones of the quay.

'It's tomorrow she's coming out then?'

'That's right,' she heard her uncle reply, 'we'll all have our hands full, that's for sure.'

Suddenly associating the trip to the hospital with her aunt, Louise felt sad. 'Will Auntie Mary be in bed, then?'

Half abstracted, her mother said, 'No jumping on the bed, now.'

Then the car stopped and her father opened the door.

'Well, well, what's the matter all of a sudden?'

Their enormous heads blocked the light. Louise saw her mother hurry off towards the door, leaving them to follow.

'She thinks it's her they'll keep in the hospital, that's it.'

Her uncle handed her a brown paper bag, indicating, with much winking to show it was a secret although her father looked uninterested, that she might help herself. They were nice grapes after all: she half hoped Auntie Mary might be too ill to have them and then they could bring them home again.

The ward was large, the beds so high that she could see right under them by bending her head a little. They were face to face with Auntie Mary and her mother before she could feel surprised at the bundle offered for admiration. 'Is it yours?' she said, and salvaged dignity only when she was let climb up on the bed and leaned giantlike over the baby, realising with a terrible triumph that she would always be his big cousin.

Louise sat tucked in beside the kitchen range all morning, her offers of help waved away again, as they drifted in one by one for their dinner, the chatter disturbed at her presence. They were all uncomfortably polite for a few minutes until the plates of food were an excuse to gather with their backs turned around the table. Glancing at the kitchen clock twice a minute, she almost screamed with relief when she heard the car grind up the track and was able to leave her seat to lift her daughter from Richard's arms. Suddenly, Aunt Mary was rushing forward to admire and exclaim in a familiar way; pleased at Richard's presence, her uncle took a bottle of Paddy from the press and poured them all large ones. Louise balanced her glass on the edge of the chair, anxious not to disturb the fragile talk of prices and drainage. She saw that Richard, with his tweeds and his sparse use of words, blended in here in an effortless transformation to which she, the rightful inheritor, had long lost the key.

Anne sat quietly on her knee for a while, delighted at the new place, the admiring strangers. Louise envied her uncritical stare at the peeling walls which she had never seen in their pristine state. Soon, she was being led out to the hens by Teddy; Louise watched them go with relief, feeling comfortably ignored for the first time, remembering suddenly that her mother had always sat in the same sagging chair, knitting or sewing as the rain beat on the windows and the children cut pictures out of the newspaper at the splintering deal table.

'Need a top-up, Louie?'

Her uncle was waving the bottle in the direction of her corner, Richard was half turned in his chair to interpret her refusal.

'Thanks. I'm fine.'

Despite her reassurance and her smile at Richard, the talk at the table halted, disrupted by her silent vigil.

'I'll be back in a minute,' she said eventually.

After she had folded her nightdress onto the top of her suitcase, Louise sat down on the low bed. From this angle, the ceiling's curves seemed to have receded into the larger perspectives of childhood and she leaned back against the wall, lulled by the familiar rise and fall of murmured voices below.

'Mind if I come in?'

Louise jumped slightly as Mary's face rounded the door.

'Oh — you're packed already.'

They stood facing each other for a moment, hunched slightly under the heavy roof, listening to the wind in the elms. At last Mary turned away and moved towards the far end of the room.

'I'd like to give you some things ... things she had. It's all yours by right.'

'No, honestly — please ....'

But Louise, when she saw the yellowing Spanish shawl billowing from the trunk, was suddenly terrified that Mary would accept her refusal.

'It's always been handed down, from eldest daughter to eldest daughter. It's yours now.'

They knelt together and touched the brittle lace and the thin watered silk. Louise felt the past rasp through her fingernails, redundant as the fragile object she had only once seen her mother wear, on the most perfect of the many perfect summer evenings. The material was now paper crisp in the warm attic, the shawl no longer wearable, merely emblematic. As she bent her head in mourning, Mary grasped her hand with warm, rough fingertips and they waited together, until Mary spoke.

'Are you sure you won't stay on a bit?... No, no, of course.'

'The swans are back again, Louie, did you know?'

As she stepped into the kitchen, her uncle and Richard were piling the glasses on the draining board. Louise looked at them in surprise.

'Swans?' she said haltingly, as though it was the first word of a foreign language she had just begun to speak again. 'You mean, down at the stream?'

'You seem to bring them back, don't you?' Richard smiled at her and suddenly she realised how much he knew about her inheritance, more than she herself knew. In his smile, she recovered the memory, lost to her conscious mind since childhood: the stream running through the bottom field, the patina of swan down on its smooth surface each spring.

'Let's go and see them, then,' she decided, smiling back at her aunt and uncle grouped with Richard by the kitchen table. The old chair creaked faintly as she rose, almost excitedly. 'Where's Anne?'

The family of swans was just visible from the top of the rise and she craned her neck, forgetting for a while her new shoes and the tightness of her tailored suit. They were not plain black as she remembered them but, especially the cygnets, a soft grey; even as she watched, the tiny handfuls of fluff struggled anxiously in the parents' wake, moving off towards the bend in the stream. As she waited for Richard to carry Anne across the field, Louise looked over her shoulder at the farmhouse, catching a glimpse of movement through the kitchen window. For a moment it occurred to her that they might all be gathered there around the table, laughing at her hobble in her town shoes just to see a few swans. But then she realised that in fact Mary was waving from the doorway of the house, tiny against the elm trees and the flat plains and she thought of her cousin, their only son, who was somewhere in Australia, planted in a different land.

As Richard and Anne caught up with her, she turned away to the stream and saw that the flotilla was almost out of sight around a bend. Behind her, Anne was panting with excitement.

'Mummy, quickly,' she called, 'show me the swans you used to know.'